Tethered
Michael Mustachio

CONTENTS

1. Old Man River — 1
2. The Shadows Know — 47
3. Off The Map — 75
4. In Season — 121

About the Author — 179

ONE
OLD MAN RIVER

It is argued that souls may only dwell within corporeal bodies. The devout go a step beyond, insisting that the dubious gift of ensoulment is further restricted. They do not inhabit indiscriminately. Only beings made in the image of specific gods are so blessed to be regarded above the lower beasts. At best, this is all conjecture. At worst, a product of fallacious reasoning. Unfortunately, all debate surrounding the existence and purpose of souls is likely to remain as far from a scientific process as a thing can be.

If souls exist, they are a magic we may not deserve. As to why anything would affix itself to something as temporary and unstable as man, that might be better left unknown. It seems just as probable that a soul would be inclined to find a home within any self-aware entity.

Rivers are such things, and all one need do is spend time close to one to realize it. They feel, and can be felt, in the most primal of ways. Sit on a quiet bank alone and you will see, and know that you are seen in return. Sometimes rivers speak – if you're the rare sort who knows how to listen. They have secrets to tell, and this river has more than most.

It is a monstrous, winding serpent of dark water, master of all things upon and within it. On a hazy day, one bank is not visible from the other. In a storm, it surges like the lifeblood of a vengeful god. On this syrupy afternoon, it is at peace, making no sound but for the vague, contented hiss that is the language of all rivers.

The air is thick with the greenish tang of life. Birds and frogs sing in the tall grasses that choke the banks. Insects buzz in the sultry air. Fish swim in her depths, eating each other and anything else unfortunate enough to fall in. Year by year, the variety of snakes increases in both number and size. This far south, alligators are everywhere – dragons lurking alarmingly close, invisible until it's too late.

All seems as it should be, and there is nobody around to suggest otherwise, when the atmosphere suddenly changes. The fauna become distinctly aware of an oddity in their midst. Ears flick. Nostrils flare. Eyes lock upon and warily monitor the approach of a large floating *thing* on the river's surface.

The object is a luxury fishing boat, the *Lazarus*, and the strange animals upon it are human men. They are utterly alien here, and as dangerous as anything that has ever existed on Earth. It is fair to say that these creatures have, on the whole, also done their share of good, but the scales have slowly and surely been tipping to the contrary.

Lazarus has been trailing a long wake of silence, now abruptly broken. Few, if any, animals here have ever heard the unnatural discord of human speech, and they flee. Flight is instinctive to most animals whenever faced with any unknown. Still, it is more appropriate just now than any of these creatures could possibly understand. Most of the wildlife scamper off immediately, taking wing, slipping deeper into the shadows of the forest, or splashing into the relative safety of the water. Even the wild boar - which fear little - will have none of it, snorting and squealing as they crash away into the thick brush.

Though intimately familiar with this river, neither of the men has ever followed it so far from civilization. They've ventured beyond the arteries and veins and well into the capillary, and both are utterly out of their depth. Moreover, they seem more than just physically out of place. They are tense, their troubled expressions telling a darker story than words alone can convey. They drift silently with the current, ignoring the fishing poles hanging over the side of the vessel like a pair of lazy antennae. The hooks are not baited. Neither Lucius nor Noah would dare eat anything pulled out of the river today - and it was the only opinion upon which they'd seen eye to eye in a long time.

Lucius owns the boat, putting it yet again to a purpose for which it was not intended. Misuse was something he did exceedingly well. Not everyone was cut out to be a hero, Lucius believed. Heroism was overrated and rarely lucrative, so once a man determined to do whatever was necessary to succeed, there was no point in half-assing things. He affirmed the notion by dumping another bucketful of thick sludge over the stern. He was *extremely* careful not to get any on his skin. Ordinarily he wore thick rubber gloves that ran up to his elbows, but he didn't want Noah to see him do that. It had been hard enough to convince him to get in the boat.

The abnormality of the dumping process was not at all like rain, and it drove most of the lingering aquatic life even farther away. The few animals that did not immediately flee were dead within seconds of coming into contact with it.

Lucius grinned like a shark at the disgusted scowl on his cousin's face as he dipped the bucket back in to rinse. He was thorough, eyeing the inside to ensure that it was pristinely orange again before dropping it to the deck. He turned about with a grand, encompassing gesture. "See?" he drawled, "no problem. Nobody comes out here." He stared until Noah met his eye, then smirked and added, "Pud." The rangy man chuckled, giving Noah a look that said *I can't believe this guy is my blood*. Noah's lack of response was uncomfortably long and loud. "We gotta dump it somewhere," Lucius finally continued, shrugging. "Sure as shit can't just toss it in the woods out behind the house."

"God forbid," Noah finally replied. "then *you* might get sick. Wouldn't want that, would we?"

With an exaggerated sigh, Lucius sank into one of the plush, swiveling deck chairs, facing Noah as he fished a beer out of the eight-hundred-dollar cooler between them. "Itoldja nobody gets sick from touching it," he said tightly. It was at least the tenth time he'd made the assertion. It would have been somewhat more believable had Noah not noticed how cautiously Lucius handled the procedure. Each time, he was as slow and mindful as a snake wrangler to avoid getting any of the substance on himself. He'd asked Lucius why he wasn't wearing gloves and gotten no response.

"We're miles from everywhere. Look." Lucius waved dismissively at the river with his free hand. "Can't even see it anymore after a bit." He downed the beer and belched, crunching the can and tossing it into the water. "Whaddayou care, anyhow?" He asked, voice thick with amusement. "Looking to buy a summer house roun' thisaway?"

"How is that relevant?" Noah snapped, watching the can spin away on the surface eddies. He looked into Lucius' face. "Did you know that the amount of water on Earth never changes?"

Lucius stared. "You just made that up."

Noah shook his head slowly, gravely, his calm hazel eyes regarding the other man from beneath the wide brim of his well-worn fisherman's hat. "It cycles over and over between liquid and vapor, but the volume stays constant. The water in this river was once in an ocean, or a lake in Asia, or the clouds. It was dinosaur piss. Realistically, it's possible that you've taken showers with the same water that Jesus Christ himself once drank."

Lucius smirked, but the expression didn't touch his eyes. Noah's words were having at least some sort of impact, so he pressed on. "People *do* come out here, Luc, and even if they didn't, water is always going somewhere else. Sooner or later, that shit's gonna make its way to where people are. Somebody's gonna wind up swimming in it. Or eating fish that got into it. Or drinking it," he finished pointedly. He felt like he was trying to explain to a hysterical toddler why his shadow won't stop following him. "Do any of your *associates* have kids?" He let his gaze wander downstream, then laughed through his nose as though what he'd said was a joke. "What a stupid question," he said, mostly to himself, "I'm sure they don't." He drummed his fingers on the top of the cooler, then added, "I hope not, anyway. But I'd bet some of them have waterfront homes." He patted the rail. "And boats."

As a rule, Noah tried not to condescend to anyone, even if they deserved it, but Luc's offhand comment about his financial situation was a deliberate slap. It was common enough knowledge that Noah had fallen on tough times... again. He didn't need to have it thrown in his face.

Almost every major financial decision he made seemed to go to shit. It bordered on statistical impossibility. *The sun should shine on a dog's ass at least once in a while*, he thought with a grimace. But the dog's ass that was Noah's life remained stubbornly dark, and desperation had finally brought him to this.

Lucius had guaranteed that getting on board would set Noah's money issues straight once and for all, and that it was mostly on the up and up. *"Get the stick outta yer ass, Noah,"* he'd said. "Nobody *plays by the rules anymore.*" Luc probably stood to make even more money out of the deal, Noah was sure. The man did nothing unless there was a dollar amount attached to it, and he'd pitched this well indeed. When Noah had climbed aboard he'd been grudgingly acknowledging that it would be a great relief to finally get his head above financial water. But this was not the way. What they were doing was *wrong*, and Noah was now part of it just by being present. 'Complicit' was the specific term a prosecutor could now use to accurately describe him.

Even if none of the blowback were ever to hit him personally, the whole experience was nauseating. The mere fact that he'd agreed to any of it was going to bother him for the rest of his days. He could already sense it forming like a core memory, certain to rise like a waterlogged carcass during any moment of honest self-reflection - a thing to which all decent people now and again subject themselves. He inhaled deeply through his nose, filling himself with the wild scent of happy summer memories. It brought him a much-needed moment of peace.

Noah knew this venture had to be a bad idea even before Lucius broached it. It was Lucius, after all. But Noah had listened anyway. Then, despite knowing better, he agreed to come along. He glanced at his cousin, who was carelessly draining yet another beer, and silently wished for a game warden to show up. Noah would catch some collateral hell, of course, but at least he wouldn't have to think of another way of preventing any more slop from going into the water.

Even as a child, something had always been off about his cousin, and the clarity of adolescence only brought Luc's behaviors into sharper focus. The onset of true adulthood had cemented it, sending them irrevocably down opposite forks in the roads of their lives. It was amazing that Luc managed to avoid prison or an untimely death. Why, Noah wondered, did adults never think to warn children that some of their relatives were fucked up? More importantly, why not advise them to steer clear? That type of education would be far more useful to any kid than quadratic equations or stories about flying reindeer.

Ultimately, Noah was here not because he wanted to be a criminal, but because he was a pushover. He'd come to terms with that fact long ago but refused to ever regard it as a character flaw. Hoping for the best in people was never a bad thing, especially where family was concerned. Now, here he was…lost on the river and fishing without bait.

This wasn't the first time he'd found himself disappointed by another's casual disregard – or even outright willingness – to do harm, and unfortunately, it wasn't likely to be the last. But Noah silently vowed that even if he wound up homeless, hell would freeze over before he would put so much as a single drop of poison into this river, or anywhere else. Furthermore, this would mark the end of him having anything to do with his cousin.

Lucius, who had been working his jaw like he had a piece of gristle stuck between his teeth, finally spoke again. "You're right, the water does go somewhere else," he spat, "but there's a lot of it, and that gives the byproduct plenty of time to get dissipated to the point where it's safe."

"Diluted," Noah said.

"What?"

"Nothing," Noah sighed. He wondered how much of the poisonous slime Lucius and his scumbag partners had already dumped. And where. As he watched the undulating slick of biological waste flow out and away, roiling like it had a life of its own, he pictured some confused emergency room resident trying to figure out what kind of poison was killing the patient twisting on the gurney before him.

As a point of fact, the stuff they were dumping *was* alive. It was a mutagenic fungus, which made it hard to estimate how dangerous it might be. That was a piece of information that Luc had wisely kept to himself until they'd been hours into the trip, of course. Otherwise, Noah would never have agreed to come. He started to reach down to let his fingers trail in the water and then thought better of it.

Noah's stomach crawled, rolling like a bunch of eels wriggling in his guts... but not nearly enough. Good people are often too trusting for their own good, and do not realize just how precarious a situation can become until it's too late. Noah couldn't have known - and did not know - just how grave his predicament was. He was oblivious to how closely he was being watched. Evaluated. Judged. The lack of awareness wasn't purposeful. He'd always been a distractable sort, a curse that often afflicts the intelligent and creative. Now he was especially so, for something was off-kilter in the river valley.

Noah was an avid outdoorsman, and more familiar with this country than most wildlife biologists. As they'd drifted farther and farther into these remote and lonely parts, he'd begun to sense that something was amiss. It didn't seem to be anything threatening, so it merely tickled at the periphery of his awareness. He concentrated on the landscape, puzzling over what was out of place. It was so subtle and gradual that when it hit him, he went rigid in his seat. It was the animals.

First, there were bird calls he couldn't put feathers to. Then the bugs were becoming more varied and much larger than they should be. At the last bend in the river there had been dragonflies as big as dinner plates, and he caught a glimpse of an orb weaver spider that looked like it could have caught a small child in its web. Now, Noah was seeing fish that he did not recognize at all, which he did not think was possible. He'd been fishing on this river with his daddy and uncles since he could hold a pole.

A sudden motion caught his attention. As if bidden, a large, misshapen form split the cattails at the near shore and jetted under the boat. As it disappeared into the darker water of the river's center, the resulting swell was enough to rock the twenty-five-foot craft. He saw Lucius glance nervously at the remaining buckets lashed to the gunwale. Noah found himself recalling that dolphins, some species of sharks, and now even *crocodiles* were reported to be navigating into North American swamps and river systems. But whatever had just passed beneath them didn't have the right shape to have been any of those things. Beyond that, he somehow just *sensed* that it was something else. He didn't know how or why he could be so sure of it, but it made him uneasy.

"Luc. Are you watching the water?" he asked distractedly.

"Whatchou yappin bout now?"

"You seeing anything strange?"

"No." A pause. "Anahwouldn'cur if I did."

"Of course you wouldn't," Noah replied flatly. *Fuck him, wait and see if something don't snatch his ass outta this boat,* he thought, and returned to scanning their surroundings. It seemed critical that he figure out what had him so on edge.

Unbeknownst to Noah, this trip was even more disappointing for Lucius. Until recently, he'd entertained no consideration of ever involving Noah in important business matters. The man was not built for it... but there was a risk versus reward aspect to this trip that Lucius could not overlook.

Noah was probably the most intelligent man Lucius had ever known, and that intellect was being squandered by bullshit ethics. Generally, Lucius didn't have any qualms about using people. Everybody was a potential resource, and that included family. The trouble was that Noah wasn't just a cousin. He was the closest thing Lucius had to a brother. They'd run the woods, hunted and fished together. They'd drunk their first beers and crushed on the same girls. It was a shame that they'd grown so far apart, although it was unlikely that it could have gone any other way. Noah had always seemed content to drift with whatever currents carried him. Lucius had set an early course that would allow him to not merely succeed, but conquer.

He studiously avoided looking at Noah as he reminisced, wishing that he'd managed to come up with a better option. Anything would have been better than bringing his cousin out here. It wasn't as though he hadn't racked his brain trying to think up something better, yet here he was.

Lucius continued to scan their surroundings for other boaters, hikers, or hunters...all potential witnesses who would have to go. His hand twitched towards the things he concealed within his clothing. He managed to catch himself, but it was close. He balled his hands into fists, grimaced, and cursed softly under his breath before forcing himself to relax.

When one made a habit of carrying illegal weapons, as Lucius always did, breaking one's self of tells was crucial. Police, in particular, were especially attentive to the body language of people who were hiding things, although packing heat wasn't something to advertise in any case. At any given time it might prove necessary to aggressively protect business interests, and it wasn't smart to *ever* alert anyone to the fact that they were about to be perforated. Lucius hadn't done any wet work in years. He'd been promoted out of it, so to speak. On the occasions when it was necessary it was never personal, and he'd never had one nightmare about any of the things he'd done. He truly never expected to have to do it again, and sure as hell not in a situation like this. Thinking about it made him a little sick to his stomach.

Lucius was a man of straight lines, and had cultivated the belief that if a person refused to use their innate gifts for gain, then it was reasonable that others should, if only to keep them from being wasted. As far as being gifted went, Noah should be a god damned millionaire by now.

Both men had endured just enough college to quit before the end of their sophomore year. Lucius recognized a scam when he saw it, and neither had cared for nor trusted the bullshit politics and virtue signaling that had replaced actual education. In Noah's case, it was the college's loss. *If only they'd known what a resource they'd had*, Lucius thought with a smirk. Noah would never need a degree to excel. He was a prodigious autodidact and possessed a flawless memory. As far back as middle school, he made some teachers nervous or uncomfortable – and even more of them jealous and angry.

Nobody likes to be proven wrong, least of all adults. Teachers, in particular, dislike being called out by students - especially in front of a class of giggling, smirking adolescents. It's even worse if the student in question is right, as Noah always was. Lucius had always considered it sort of an odd contradiction in his cousin. He was well-behaved and compliant to a fault in most situations, yet he never gave an inch of ground when he knew he was in the right.

Noah could hold his own, and then some, on any subject from fine art and design to the intricacies of string theory and molecular biology. Most importantly, he wasn't one of those smart guys whose intellect was a hindrance in any way - like the tedious, spindly social misfits whom Lucius had always loved to torment. Noah was charming and funny, and a genius at finding creative solutions to complex problems. Plus, he was a treasure trove of useless knowledge, and often pulled things out of his ass that he had no business knowing. He was virtually a human Google when it came to trivia in general, and a menace at recalling things like movie references and song lyrics. Lucius recalled once when they'd been together at a dorm party playing a drinking version of Trivial Pursuit. It was men versus women, and Noah had been asked what material women's corsets had been made of. The girls had been smugly certain that no man could hope to know such a thing, but Lucius never had a doubt. Noah had answered like a gunslinger: *whalebone*.

"How in the hell could you *possibly* know that?" Somebody had asked. Noah paused, swigged his beer like he was holstering a smoking revolver, and replied "That was a *biology* question, not a *fashion* question. And it came from baleen whales, by the way."

The ability to apply knowledge in such a shrewd and timely manner was a rare, priceless gift. It was why Noah was out here with him today, and the reason why Lucius had begun, many years prior, to hamstring his cousin - one striation at a time. It was ironic that, intelligent as he was, the man never realized he was being kept in a stable.

It was just good business to catch and hold onto things… especially people, until their usefulness was recognized, nurtured and fully exploited. Life was precious, but to predators of Lucius' caliber it was also a commodity. Lucius Strahan was like a spider in his associations, except that he did not kill the unfortunates who blundered into his web. Not too soon, at least; there was nothing to be gained in killing something prematurely if it could be bled indefinitely.

He had determined long ago to keep Noah close - at the center of the web, so to speak - so that he could be properly cultivated. Lucius could never have guessed, however, that it would prove to be the wisest decision he'd ever made. Noah had become the crown jewel of Lucius' collection. He was probably doing Noah a favor, to be honest. If the man insisted on refusing to realize his own value, somebody else was bound to. It was only a matter of time and odds. Lucius, at least, would try to avoid harming him in the process. It was going to depend on whether or not Noah could be reasonable.

He gazed momentarily at his cousin's exposed back and neck, expression carefully veiled as though Noah might suddenly look his way and somehow see him for what he was. If Lucius had ever found himself in such a grave situation, he would have already recognized it. Not only would he have extricated himself by now, but probably also devised a way to turn it to his advantage. But Lucius did not blunder into anything. Not ever.

He grinned at his reflection, distorted in the river he was currently spoiling, then dumped another case of beers into the cooler. Noah didn't even twitch at the sound. *Off in his own world again.* Lucius shook his head slowly and nudged the other's elbow with a beer, which Noah took without looking. *What a shame.* Noah probably still believed that it had been his decision to come on this little excursion. But that wasn't true at all.

For those willing, it was a simple matter to gain leverage over others, provided those "others" were conveniently decent... or stupid. Lucius avoided the latter in general, of course. Aside from finding their company distasteful, there was little or no sport in manipulating idiots, and often no financial gain.

Kind people weren't as easy to manipulate, but there was usually something to show for the effort. Everyone Lucius had left behind in his former life, and basically all of his family, were both kind *and* decent - and that was their problem. It was said that kindness should not be mistaken for weakness, but Lucius disagreed. If that adage were true, old people would never get fucked out of their life savings by telemarketing scams, which happened every day. Too often, gentle people didn't notice the sheep's clothing until the wolf had its jaws around their throat. Even worse, sometimes they refused to even acknowledge that wolves existed at all.

People had tried to run games on him in the past, and in each case he'd unleashed hell upon them. "Turning the other cheek" was the real weakness, and it was a quality that Lucius loathed.

Crushing the successful and affluent, however, was a rush; even better if the mark was brilliant. Intelligent people were always valuable in one way or another, but it didn't have to be about money. His manipulation of Noah was a perfect example. Lucius had discovered that capitalizing upon an intelligent person for a penny's worth of profit was infinitely more gratifying than making millions from a moron. It was an accomplishment. Lucius' mentors in the Org proved as much. Jian's path to success was paved with the crushed bones of Forbes list entrepreneurs, and Khan had become Lucius' personal Sith Lord in his tutelage of the dark art of acquiring wealth. Their personalities were as different as could be, but both men were predators of the highest order.

At a certain point, money ceased to be a concern; there was only so much stuff a person could need or use. Once an individual secured generational wealth, the art of business transcended material gain, and became the game of games. Lucius discovered early in life that he loved to play it.

Lucius based his worldview of humanity, oddly enough, on a tee-shirt he'd once seen as a kid, which read: *There are three kinds of people; those who make things happen, those who watch things happen, and those who wonder what happened.*

It was only mildly amusing at the time, but for some reason the image had stuck with him. It was like an awkward piece of furniture in the darkness of his subconscious. He knew it was there, but still stubbed the shit out of his brain on it once in a while. Ironically, the less he thought about it the more harmful it seemed, and it was odd how prophetic that slogan had proven itself to be. On a fundamental but significant level, every person belonged to one of those three types. Although - as Lucius would come to learn - there was only one that mattered: The Makers. It wasn't their actual name, of course. He doubted that they had one. A group that powerful wouldn't need a fancy title.

The Makers were the small group of insanely wealthy people who actually ran the world. It was an age-old conspiracy theory, and one which had always seemed preposterous to Lucius. He'd since learned, and in the worst possible way, that it was all too real. Even for someone as jaded as he, the bombshell revelation blew his mind. Still, it had seemed largely irrelevant. A man like Lucius could never be a player at that level; it was one of those social stations a person must be born into. He reckoned that the designs of the Makers would never adversely affect him or his business affairs, so long as he stayed off their radar and played by the rules - such as they were. That presumption was, after all, the cornerstone of the business that he and his partners were working so hard to build. How naive he'd been.

Most everyone else - Watchers, Wonderers or otherwise - was insignificant, and useful only because they served the necessary function of keeping the wheels of commerce rotating. The masses were like the bugs and feeder fish in this river; nothing more than food that kept bigger, more interesting things alive. Lucius had always felt that way about other people; an outlook that amused him before he discovered that he, himself, was only a little higher on the food chain.

Then there were people like Noah; brilliant, capable, kind, and over-conscientious. Crusaders. They didn't merely acknowledge issues and problems; they always wanted to make things better. Noah, in particular, was the kind of guy who pulled over to help somebody change a flat tire in the rain. Lucius lost count of how many times he'd seen his cousin go out of his way for complete strangers. He was a man who would willingly suffer for the benefit of others who might never know or care.

In short, Noah was the type of person who ought to be running the world, but people like him simply weren't greedy enough to ever become powerful. Noah was, quite literally, too decent a person for his own good.

Lucius had no such confrontations, and did not want them. Utter waste of mental energy. He believed in control. The world only made sense when you forced it to, and that was a fact. Lucius controlled the lives of those around him to an almost unimaginable degree, including many of his own family members. None were even remotely aware of it. His own parents had no idea that the bank that owned the mortgage to their home was, in turn, owned by Lucius. He'd purchased it over a decade ago. He still borrowed money from them to this very day just to keep up appearances.

The idea that he owned a bank still amazed him sometimes – and his wealth paled compared to what was possible. Several of the highest-ranking superiors in the Organization had amassed personal fortunes that surpassed the gross national product of some foreign countries. But where Lucius had once aspired to one day be at their level, he now hoped to still be alive in five years to enjoy what he'd accomplished. Coming out here to Bumfuck on this humid day to slap at mosquitoes in one last effort to get his cousin to play ball was the least of it. He would expend every last resource to that end.

Lucius had always swum in the deepest, darkest waters of society and business. He fit right in with the creatures that one expected to find in such environments, and had quickly become acquainted with some of the Organizations scouts. He'd risen quickly and steadily in the ranks and become an asset to all the right people. He was quite satisfied with his progress and growing status – until he'd learned of the plot that had tilted his world off its axis. Even now, he could scarcely process it.

It all revolved around Tether Corporation, golden child of international business, whose global philanthropy touched even small, backwater communities like theirs. They could rightly be counted as Makers, but they were playing the game at a level that wasn't supposed to be possible. Tether was planning a hostile takeover. That, in itself, would come as no surprise to anyone who understood how the corporate world worked. Cutthroat tactics were necessary to survive – not that Lucius cared or was in any position to judge… but this was to be no simple financial coupe.

As Lucius understood it, Tether's top leadership had formed a small, intimate faction who referred to themselves as the Consiglieri. While high-level cliques were typical in virtually every powerful organization, it was safe to say that few were currently planning to seize control of the entire world. And that was *precisely* what this Council intended.

Tether absolutely had the resources, and there were probably a lot of people who might even welcome the intervention. Governments could scarcely fuck things up worse than they had for pretty much all of the preceding century, while Tether had probably done more good than any entity in human history. Not even a pessimist like Lucius could argue that point. The problem wasn't necessarily *that* they would attempt such a thing. The problem was *how* they were planning to go about it. The Council wanted the world – but not its people.

It was Laura who'd told him. Like all of his intimate relationships, theirs had been limited to the physical.

They'd had a long, marathon night together and she'd dropped it on him the next morning. At first, Lucius dismissed the entire tale as ridiculous. His first reaction had been to actually laugh in her face... until he realized that she'd been physically sick with terror. By the time she'd finished telling him all she knew, so was he. He supposed that she had to tell someone – it wasn't the type of information that wanted to stay secret. Regardless, Lucius would never understand why the fuck she thought it would be a good idea to share such a dangerous secret with someone like *him*.

She'd flatly refused to tell him how she knew, and he didn't want to believe any of it; but it made too much sense to be bullshit. He'd stewed over it for a few days, as people tend to do with bad news, slowly trying to convince himself that it had been a misunderstanding on Laura's part. Then she'd disappeared. Lucius had known immediately that that she would never be seen again. In his world, any time a person suddenly went missing, one must always assume the worst. Her disappearance not only dispelled any lingering doubts he'd harbored about the veracity of her claims, but it also increased his dread to a petrifying level.

Like many powerful entities, the Council didn't technically exist. Groups of this sort did not send emails or have board meetings, but they had the resources to protect their anonymity by any means necessary. The moment he was certain Laura was gone for good, Lucius went to ground. He spent two sleepless days hiding, transiting through the many vacant properties he owned. Fortified with enough coffee to enliven a corpse and an arsenal of illegal weapons, he'd prowled from window to window, waiting for the inevitable. It could only be a question of time before he was snipped off as another loose end.

On the third day, he concluded that the Council didn't know about him. It was the only thing that made sense. If they had, he wouldn't have lasted one day, much less three. There had never been a net that could catch every fish, and Lucius had gotten lucky. Plus, he'd had no choice but to go back to business as usual; he couldn't afford to arouse the suspicion of his own people on top of everything else. The Council might eventually find him, and if they did, all of the grenades and automatic rifles in the world were not going to save him.

Days crept into a series of crawling weeks. In the end he endured several long, agonizing months of looking over his shoulder every thirty seconds before he started to relax. Looking back, those had been some of the most stressful moments of his entire life... but it cracked open a door of sorts, giving him a glimpse of new possibilities.

Ultimately, Lucius didn't care how people made their money so long as it didn't disrupt his own personal interests. The Council's operational plan definitely qualified as disruptive. According to Laura, Phase One was genocide.

A predetermined number of people were designated to survive this purge. Not only would they have to be prodigiously intelligent and share the Council's ambition, but also willing to stand by and witness the murder of almost every human being on the planet. *Billions* of people did not fall into the category of survivors, and it didn't take a great deal of imagination for Luc to know which group he was in. Of equal concern was that Laura had no idea when this Transition was due to happen. Lucius was sure that it would be sooner than anyone would like.

Lucius knew enough about technology to realize everything Laura had divulged was one hundred percent possible. He'd come to believe that the one person most likely to ensure his own survival was Noah.

This boat trip was no routine dump run that any low-ranking white-trash gofer could do. It was an assessment. Lucius had been taking periodic water samples via a small gauge trailing behind the boat. It was absolutely imperative that the dispersal rate of the dross was rapid enough to prevent detection even in slow-moving bodies of water. He'd been transmitting the data back to the Org via bio-encryption. As he understood it, the folks at NSA were pulling out their hair trying to hack it.

Lucius was about to take a big step up in the Org. It was the equivalent of becoming a made man in the mafia, but better. It was a much more stable outfit. Should the Tether apocalypse prove to be bullshit, or fail - and either of those scenarios was possible - Lucius would find himself well-positioned to become a very wealthy man, and better protected than a U.S. Congressman. At the very least, the promotion might give him the clout to get Noah in, and keep them both safe as he maneuvered his way into Tether's safe harbor. It would be good to bring someone he trusted along, someone from his former life to keep with him as he climbed to prestige. Family.

In the meantime, Lucius was going to proceed as if the apocalypse was a genuine existential threat. His plan was to become an asset to these Consigilieri, and it wasn't going to be easy. It was critical that Lucius stay off the Council's radar while working to insinuate himself.

In order to get close enough to them, he had to first become part of Tether. Unfortunately for Lucius, Tether did not need him… and likely never would. Simply put, Lucius was not smart enough to be of any real value. He wasn't bothered by the admission. He was a realist, and pragmatic to a fault. That's where Noah came in.

Lucius stretched and cracked another beer. Noah might already have been picked up by Tether or someone like them had it not been for Lucius' own interventions. Still, that was easy to remedy. Tether was known to actively headhunt talent. It would take little or no effort to shine Noah right on up and dangle him where those Consiglieri would be sure to notice.

If Noah made it in, there was a chance that Luc could be grandfathered in - like a "plus one" on an invite to the ultimate post-game blowout. He eyed Noah critically, very aware of the man's growing agitation. Like his namesake, Noah would be the captain of Luc's lifeboat; otherwise they were both dead men. But for any of it to work, Noah had to be made to take the critical first step. He had to play ball, and things were not looking good.

So far, in spite of Lucius' maneuvering and coaxing, his cousin had not dumped a single bucket of the byproduct. He shouldn't be surprised; when they were kids Noah wouldn't even steal candy bars. What could he possibly say to convince such a person that the world was about to end? *Yeah, so you know the Tether Corporation, right? Well, they're gonna murder billions of people all over the world. Not sure when, but it's probably gonna be soon. So what I'm gonna need you to do is help me survive that by getting in good with the people at the top. You'll have get a job with my people first, of course, and you'll have to prove yourself by dumping the rest of this poisonous shit into this river.* Lucius pictured that conversation and then actually laughed out loud. He expected Noah to look around, but the man's attention remained on the river. *What*, Lucius wondered, *could possibly be so interesting?*

It was never going to be an easy task, but he'd managed to get his cousin this far. He knew Noah as well as anybody, and knew just what to do. He'd reeled him in slowly and patiently, teasing him with hints about the scientific aspects of what the Organization was actually doing. He fabricated a false narrative that the Org had a positive pharmacological benefit, knowing it would prove irresistible. And he'd been right.

He considered just telling his cousin the truth, but what if Noah refused? *Refuse? What if he snitched?* Could Lucius really trust him to keep it to himself? If the DEA ever discovered what the Org was up to, it would result in a lengthy, unpleasant, and undoubtedly rapey stay in one of the country's finer federal penal institutions. There were a lot to choose from, any of which would be more than happy to make room for Lucius and his partners.

The only bright side to this scenario was that incarceration would prove short. Once his colleagues discovered that it was Lucius' boy scout cousin who'd dimed them all out - and they *would* figure it out - not even solitary confinement would protect him from being literally skinned alive. That excruciating end wouldn't be as short as he would hope, but it would at least keep him from rotting in jail for the remainder of his natural life.

As for the Council, those psychopaths would murder the two of them, their families and friends, and even their pets. Hell, they would burn down an entire city to keep their plan for world domination from being revealed. Lucius was certain of that because he would do at least that much to protect his own interests.

In the end he had no choice. Lucius was never one to just give up on anything. In this case the alternative to doing nothing was to fall, along with the stupid, bleating human cattle, under Tether's scythe. And there was no telling what that end might be like. One could hope that Tether's judgment would not be as severe as a flaying, given their vast body of good work, but the worst-case scenario couldn't be ruled out. If their capacity for harm equaled that of their benevolence... it was terrifying to consider.

As for Noah, he wouldn't have known that his fate was being weighed even if he'd looked right into Lucius' eyes. The wheels of his cousin's thought processes spun quietly, well-greased by money and blood, and kept efficiently running by an adamantine sense of self-preservation.

On the flip side of the familial coin, Noah's heart was the captain of his soul. He and Lucius had grown up on this river together. They'd played in its shallows, fished the depths, and caught critters. Noah had lost his virginity to a gorgeous dark-eyed bayou siren on this very river. It had happened during a warm spring rain under the canopy of a giant weeping willow. As he recalled, it hadn't been an occasion for weeping at all, and the recollection brought a wistful grin to his otherwise troubled face.

Then he noticed that remnants of whatever Lucius was dumping continued to roil tenaciously in the current behind the boat, and a scowl slapped the smile clean away. The substance steamed a bit in the cool water, and when the wind shifted, it carried the odd, sickly sweet funk of the brew with it. Ultimately, Noah didn't care what people did to themselves as long as it didn't hurt others, but that was exactly what was happening here. Nothing was worth this putting down roots in his conscience. He may never become materially wealthy, but his ethics and morals had always been beyond reproach, and he intended to keep it that way. He was lucky that he could still back out.

Of all the things this "opportunity" could have been, Noah was shocked to learn that it involved drugs. He glanced at Lucius, who was eyeing the goo in the other buckets as if he were considering dipping a finger in and tasting it. The man was slick as an alley cat when at social interaction, but had always been something of a slacker in formal education. He was by no means dumb, but it was unlikely that he understood the magnitude of how dangerous this was.

In the neighboring worlds of chemistry and biology there wasn't much that Noah couldn't follow. The specifics of what the waste material was, precisely, would be beyond the intellectual grasp of anyone without a PhD. Based upon what he'd gleaned from Lucius about the refined drug, it was more like alchemy. That being the case, the substance they were dumping had to be toxic as hell.

For all her strength, Nature could be alarmingly fragile. Introducing any biological unknown could be catastrophic to an ecosystem, and people never learned the lesson. Noah recalled how, many years ago, an Asian doctor had smuggled Snakehead fish into the States, hoping they would be beneficial in curing his terminally ill wife. When they failed to provide any holistic benefit, he released the highly aggressive fish into a stream near his home, where they thrived. The tenacious sons of bitches could actually *walk* short distances overland to get where they wanted to go, for Christ's sake, and quickly became an invasive plague that were tearing the waterways up and down the east coast a new asshole. It was probably never meant to be malicious, but it didn't matter. It never mattered. Ignorance of the mechanics of nature was no defense for the damage that was done.

But ignorance wasn't Lucius' problem. The problem was that he was just smart enough to be dangerous. He was shrewd and conniving and did not care about consequences unless they affected him directly. No great giver of fucks was his cousin when it came to trivial matters like ecology and stewardship of the planet, and the life that depended so heavily on Her wellbeing.

They'd been close as children, but as far back as Noah could remember, Luc had always gravitated towards the material. He'd always had to have the best of everything, and all means to that end were acceptable. He never thought twice about lying, cheating, or outright stealing to get what he wanted.

Lucius had money now, and a great deal more of it than he let on if this boat was any indication. Some of their kin debated as to how he came by such things without having an actual job. Lucius professed to be a consultant. Noah had long suspected that he was instead a criminal of one kind or another, and this little "fishing trip" finally confirmed it.

Noah had been daydreaming and was surprised to see his own hand trailing in the water. He thought of snatching it out, but it didn't make much sense to do so now. If the stuff had gotten on his skin, it was probably already too late to do anything about it. Still, he was relieved to see that there no longer seemed to be any around the boat.

Southern rivers can be surprisingly cool, even in the dog days of August, and the water had a calming effect on him despite the chaos in his head. He finally pulled his hand out of the current and peered at Lucius only to find him digging brazenly in his nose. Noah wiped his hands on his shorts and shook his head. They passed into another shallows where the water was so clean that he could see the sandy bottom ten feet down. He could almost feel the slow cloud of it sifting through his fingers, and he got the sudden urge to jump overboard and swim down to touch it. Under other circumstances he might just have done so, but as it happened, the water around the boat was tainted by something biological.

Things had seemed so much easier when he was young. Even though the details of those memories were starting to blur around the edges, Noah felt that his appreciation for those carefree days grew with each passing year. Like most people, he became increasingly conscious of the trials of adult life. He acknowledged that there would be concessions, but becoming a criminal was not an option. It was unthinkably corrosive, like he was being asked to sell his mother's soul.

Lucius had never used drugs, recreationally or otherwise, and as far as Noah knew, he still didn't. He'd didn't even smoke, and rarely drank. He was not surprised that Lucius had chosen a life of crime, but he couldn't fathom how his cousin could have become involved in something this bad.

Still, it was no shock that crime had found Lucius. The man might not be Mensa material nor terribly imaginative, but he was a worker, and definitely knew how to keep a secret. Both, especially the latter, were valuable traits to any employer - but probably even more so in the world of organized crime. One of them had been bound to recognize his abilities and lack of morals and make him an offer he couldn't refuse.

All of that notwithstanding, Noah still wasn't sure that Lucius wasn't bullshitting him about the details. Even given the rapid pace of science and discovery, the entire premise was hard to believe.

Someone had found yet another way for people to get high; not surprising, considering the drug trade was among the most lucrative business models in history. The industry made unfathomable sums of money providing drugs to people who would always want it. Noah recalled that Pablo Escobar had had enough money to build his own prison. But, like any big business, narcotics had its share of problems.

First of all, drugs were probably more dangerous than they'd ever been, and it was getting worse. Fentanyl, in particular, was currently killing shitloads of "customers" worldwide. The suppliers didn't care, of course, except that it shortened the clientele base. But law enforcement agencies could no longer ignore the catastrophic loss of life, and they were tightening the noose. Then, there was the unforeseen phenomenon of the legalization of substances that never should have been illegal to begin with. Between those two factors, there was a real possibility that the existing cartels could become extinct. To avoid that fate, they would have to adapt - and be allowed to do so.

Lucius' associates - a group he referred to as The Org - were actively trying to prevent that. And they were succeeding. It was that specific angle that put Noah on the river today. The Org was going to eradicate the cartels, Luc had said, and replace them. They intended to become future of organized crime, and their plan was unprecedented. Noah, in spite of his general horror, could not help but grudgingly admit to himself that it was brilliant. They were creating addicts out of people who would never willingly become them.

The scheme far surpassed what any decent person would consider evil. It was diabolical. And that was really saying something, Noah thought, considering the sad history of peoples' disregard for their fellow humans. According to Lucius, the Org's coupe was well underway, and it was already too late to stop.

Two years ago, the Org had engineered a fungus called mychosubdermachromis, MSC for short among the chemists, and bestowed the acronym MOSAIC by its aficionados and practitioners. The organism was designed to grow and spread beneath the dermis and epidermis – forming intricate, beautiful patterns as it did so.

Essentially, it was a living tattoo that grew indefinitely. Noah had seen it himself, and his fascination was what had ultimately gotten him to come along in the first place. The variations in color, shape, and texture depended upon the host's diet, race, and other subtle and untraceable factors. For young adults worldwide, and particularly American youth, it could not possibly have been more exotic. It was almost as though new races were being born, and a new counter-subculture to go with it.

They called themselves Chromags, and social media was inundated with pages dedicated to them. It was one of the wildest, coolest things Noah had ever seen. But today he'd learned that MOSAIC had a nasty secret, and it was so horrible that he was already trying to figure out how to alert the right people before it became an epidemic.

Since the organism was alive, it had to eat, and did so by feeding on keratin. This in itself was not a big deal, biologically speaking. The human body had keratin to spare, and any loss due to MOSAIC development was negligible as the growths, or blooms as they were called, had a side benefit of acting as an internal sunscreen. Nothing but beneficial, right? Wrong.

As MOSAIC developed, it began to stealthily tap into the nervous system, producing powerful endorphins that would eventually make the euphoria of heroin high pale in comparison. When the fungus began gradually providing this to its human host, it simultaneously slowed its feeding on the keratin and began to require other nourishment. That 'nourishment' came in the form of a topical or intravenous 'enhancement' that encouraged diversity of the bloom. If it was denied, MOSAIC would stop producing endorphins. Instead, it then began excreting a toxin.

Once hooked, the enhancement that the fungus required could be tailored to elicit specific reactions, providing the high. It would be twice as expensive as medical-grade cocaine, but people would do anything to literally feed the kaleidoscopic monkeys on their backs.

There were Chromags who had already experienced this downside. Luc said that they described withdrawal as being simultaneously electrocuted and burned from the inside out. The Org was collecting as many of the victims as possible under the guise of being treated for the 'rare, adverse allergic reaction.' They were being treated by semi-legit medical staff... in hospitals owned by the Org itself. There had been deaths, successfully hushed thus far. The victims screamed all the way to their last breath.

Lucius had commented casually that it could take days for that to happen. It was sporadic, as they were still in what the Org considered the "free trial phase." Further, he assured Noah that whatever was causing the premature deaths would be edited out of the MOSAIC code, as if that made it all okay. What Noah took away from it was that traumatic death was bad – only in that it proved detrimental to the Organization's bottom line.

It blew Noah's mind that brilliant people could be complicit in such cruelty, and even more so that the average American was so quick to experiment with an unknown quantity. And the developers were as creative as they were clever.

The incidents of death were not widely known, and would never be linked either MOSAIC or the Org. Luc cheerfully assured him that they were well insulated against any blowback. When Noah questioned how they could possibly keep something like that a secret, Lucius only laughed, saying that the Org's doings were nothing compared to the things the governments and legitimate corporations were up to. They were gladiators in the arena of victimization and capitalizing on the masses. *What if this Org found a way to get these tattoos into people who didn't want them?* Noah thought with a shudder.

What Noah couldn't figure out was why Lucius had chosen to divulge as much as he had. And why now? Even if he thought Noah would ever agree to be a part of all of it, what did Lucius think he could possibly bring to the table?

So here Noah was, reeling from the societal time bomb that had been dropped in his lap. He was floating along in a hundred and fifty-thousand dollar fishing boat with one of the individuals responsible for generating this misery - and that person expected him to help dump the evidence into the river and profit from it. *Does Lucius not know me at all?* He grimaced and gave a quick shake of his head, like a horse trying to rid itself of biting flies.

A breeze gusted across the water, stitching the surface in striations of sparkling light, as if the river had gotten a sudden case of goosebumps. Noah normally took great pleasure in the simple magic of it, but now he didn't even notice. Nor was he aware of the continuing changes in the physiology of the animals around them. Had he not been so distracted, he might have noticed that the fish had gone somewhat cretaceous in appearance, things of teeth and sinew and armor plate. They didn't belong to this world, and hadn't since time out of memory. Crayfish the size of jet skis crept along the bottom, claws open and waiting. The turtles, in particular, would have been enough to make a person scream. If either of the men were to go over the side, neither would be likely to surface again.

Lucius removed the trolling motor, and the boat was taken by the current, off the river proper and down a smaller fork. It was significantly narrower than the main channel, canopied by branches from the old-growth forest to either side.

He no longer knew where they were, but the important thing was that they were now well out of cell tower range. He'd checked the coverage for this area long ago in case he ever needed to make something disappear, or do so himself. It grew cooler and the living air pressed in, clinging tightly to the cousins. A mist began to skim across the surface of the water, playing about the hull in small cyclones. The trees seemed to lean in, as if trying to listen in on a private conversation. Or perhaps merely watching the men.

Noah breathed deeply, trying to draw a measure of comfort from the sudden coolness, when a change in the lapping murmur of the water caught his attention. Something enormous was splitting the current somewhere just ahead. It sounded like a rapids, which should not be. It grew increasingly louder, and he squinted into the haze to find the source. A shape began to materialize, rising high out of the roiling mist. Noah scowled at it in confusion.

A landform of some sort, it seemed - but it was unnatural. Islands and bars were commonplace on the river. They came and went, sculpted at the whims of current and storm. They varied in size, but always formed flat - the currents allowed for nothing else. But this formation looked to Noah as if a boulder had rolled down a mountainside - or a meteor had smashed into the river. Neither of these scenarios was remotely possible. A space rock of this size would have destroyed everything within a thousand miles in any direction, and there were no mountains within a hundred miles. It was remotely possible that the river itself had birthed it from somewhere deep within mud and silt, but Noah had never seen or heard of such a thing this far to the south. The hair on his arms was standing on end, and the chill he felt in the air now seemed to have no business whatsoever in a Louisiana summer.

The metallic spit of yet another beer can interrupted Noah's reverie, followed by Lucius's disruptive, unwelcome voice. "The next bucket is yours, poontang." He said, nudging the orange Home Depot bucket with his foot. Noah had never known another man to have such an extensive lexicon of vulgar references for female genitalia.

"Yeah? Don't think so," Noah replied, watching the monolith grow ever closer. "Not this time, and not ever agin," Noah finished, his irritation bringing his accent to the surface.

"Purdy much figgered that out fer m'silf." Lucius sniffed from behind. He'd made a decision. There'd been an odd flicker of a smile on Noah's face earlier. Lucius wasn't sure what it meant, but it put his back up, and instinct told him to assume the worst. Not only would Noah never get on board, he would definitely go to the authorities – even if he had to implicate himself.

Lucius had no illusions about how he was regarded by most of his kin, and even though he'd chosen this life more willingly than any of them could imagine, he still cared for some of them. There were a few that he wouldn't piss on if they were on fire. But he loved Noah. That was no small thing to a person like Lucius. *Fucking dammit.* He tossed another can over the side, started composing himself for what needed to be done, and then paused. Maybe, just maybe, Noah could be made to swear not to go running off at the mouth about the operation. Unlike himself, Noah could keep a promise. And if Noah did so, Lucius would let it go.

"Have a beer, cousin." He said, tapping Noah on the shoulder with an ice-cold can. Noah took this one also without a glance, lost in thought as he gazed at the river. Lucius was suddenly overcome by an unwelcome pang of regret. At any time in the last decade, he could have given Noah money to start a legitimate business and waited to see if there was a way he could benefit from his success somewhere down the line. And he could have done so a hundred times over.

Noah was an innocent in many ways, and there was a shortage of that in the world. But Lucius had vouched for him and done so to some extremely dangerous people. He looked hard at his cousin, who was peering into the depths of the river with childlike wonder. He saw the world so differently than anybody else Lucius knew. *Tell him the truth, goddammit!* At that moment, he almost did. Then he remembered who he was dealing with. It would never happen. Lucius' expression slowly hardened, like cold honey running down from his hairline. He rubbed at the stubble on his chin.

Noah was a good person - a legitimately good person - and good people could not be bought. They did not become part of criminal operations, willingly or through coercion, and they would never keep quiet about a plot to commit mass murder. Who had Lucius thought he'd been kidding to ever believe otherwise?

He began steeling himself for the inevitable. Lucius could not possibly know it, but he was very like a special operations soldier in that he did not suffer nightmares or PTSD. Unlike all other past incidents, however, he was going to feel this. The best he could do was make it as easy as possible for both of them. If anyone deserved to die quickly and painlessly, it was Noah.

There were no logistical concerns. Even if somebody heard the shot, none would give it a passing thought. Shooting things for no apparent reason was country as hell. People slept through it. Recreational use of explosives was even a thing in way out places where they pumped in sunshine. It wasn't the safest or smartest hobby, but still common enough to be disregarded.

Choosing this area was an absolute necessity - Lucius' .45 carried was as good as dynamite for close-up work, and damn near as loud. Anything in .45 caliber might as well be a howitzer for the effect it had on flesh and bone. The awful, gruesome part was that he was probably going to have to puncture Noah's body, then weigh it down before dumping him over the side. The corpse might float away before the things in the river could do away with the remains. If it showed up outside somebody's dock there would be questions. A part of him that could not be ignored assured him that there would be nightmares, and he believed it. He deserved at least that. But business was business.

Lucius took a long look at the back of his cousin's head. Noah was thinking his very last thoughts as a living, breathing person, and Lucius wondered offhandedly what they were. He hoped they were happy ones.

Noah, on the other hand, was growing more confused with each passing second - although not due to any of Lucius' sketchy behavior. The landmass they were approaching was even bigger than it first seemed. He cocked his head curiously. It unsettled him for some reason, and he was trying to decide why when a heron the size of a small airplane glided out of from a break in the trees. Noah's mouth dropped open. It had to be twenty feet from wingtip to wingtip. He craned his neck as it flew directly overhead, and looked as though it meant to land on the little island. At the last second it cried out in the strange guttural croak that was the heron's call, then banked sharply away. Noah watched it disappear from sight.

He couldn't even manage to say anything to Lucius, and before he could decide to do so, they were almost upon the rock. There were no trees upon it, nor vegetation of any sort. This far down south, plants grew *everywhere*. They would root and snake their way up inside metal signposts, sprout from the wheels of derelict cars – even the crotches of other trees. Once, he'd found a small maple growing out of a forgotten birdhouse inside his uncle's barn. A shaft of light, just a sliver once or twice a day, had been enough to give it hope.

The island was...chunky looking. He grinned madly, and nearly laughed out loud. It begged to be explored, and he had to restrain himself from jumping out of the boat. Then he noticed the turtles, and his breath caught in his throat.

There were *hundreds* of them, perhaps thousands. The water churned as they bumped into one another on the surface and jockeyed for position around the island. There were more than he'd ever collectively seen in his entire life, so many that it seemed he could have walked to shore on their backs. And some of them were enormous. Finally he found his tongue, and was about to mention the oddity to Lucius when the other's voice shattered the silence.

"HO! LEE! SHIT!" Lucius whooped, coming to his feet and pointing. "Would you look at the *size* of the fucking thing!" He finished with breathless amazement.

Noah could only follow his cousin's gaze to what looked like another sandbar. Noah gaped. It was an alligator snapper - the absolute king of all turtles - and this one was easily twice as big as the hood of his father's old Cadillac. A rational part of his brain informed him that this animal had to be at least three hundred years old to have grown so large.

Lucius' voice distracted him. "This sumbitch is getting towed back with me. Watch this shit," he said. When Noah looked, Lucius was holding an absolute cannon of a pistol. *Of course he's armed*, Noah thought, *he's a criminal*. He was going to kill it. NO! The word sounded bright red in his mind, and before he could think to stop himself, he was going for the gun. Lucius' face registered a flicker of surprise, then went hard and cold like a death mask. Time seemed to slow to almost nothing. The .45 swung in Noah's direction.

Then something slammed into the boat. Noah was thrown from his seat, careened into Lucius, and both men stumbled over the cooler, which toppled, spilling ice and beer cans all around their feet. Noah went down hard. There was a bright flash, and the impossibly loud, jarring eruption of the pistol. Noah's head slammed onto the deck and everything went black.

A metallic noise roused him - *chik-chik* - the unmistakable sound of a round being chambered. Something warm and wet had run into Noah's eyes, and when he wiped it away, his hand came away sticky. He knew immediately that he was lying on the deck of Lucius' boat. Above him, Cygnus and the Great Square of Pegasus were just becoming visible in the sky. Lucius stepped into view, blocking them out. He still looked resolute, but sorrowful as well.

"You know, it's a bad idea to attack someone in a boat, especially when they're holdin a gun," he said matter-of-factly, then looked away. Turtle shells continued to knock against the hull like a drumroll. "Fuck, Noah. I wish you hadn't woke up. Why can't you ever do what's in your best interest?"

Noah wasn't sure what he was talking about. Disoriented and dizzy, he wondered if he was drunk. *How many beers did I have?* He tried to stand and failed, stumbling against the side of the boat. He squinted up at Lucius. "Did you kill that turtle?"

Lucius paused, cocked his head. "What?"

"The snapper. I heard shots. Did you shoot it?"

Lucius looked at him for a long moment. "I shot *at* it," he finally said. "I don't think that I could've missed if I'd tried. Dunno if it's dead." He shrugged. "It's gone. Alligator snappers are tough as hell." A sliver of moon was just visible over behind him, vague against the dark tapestry of the heavens. The image seemed to stretch endlessly and would revisit Noah for the rest of his life...but only in dreams that he would never remember. Finally, Lucius sniffed. "Doesn't matter. In about three seconds, you won't have to worry about turtles or anything else anymore."

The barrel of any gun appears enormous when close up, and it wasn't the kind of thing a person forgot. Noah was about to be murdered by his own blood, but at that moment he didn't find it all that interesting. He was riveted by an immense darkness lifting from the water behind his cousin. *Thunderstorm?* He thought distractedly. *We should get off - too dangerous to stay on the river in a storm.*

It took Noah a moment to realize that it was the island, silhouetted against the rising blanket of night over Lucius' shoulder. It looked like a great big turtle shell... and it was moving. "Daaaamn iffat ain't a big ole' summabitch." He said aloud.

It proved just enough to distract Lucius from applying the necessary last ounce of pressure to the trigger. The barrel dipped slightly. Noah was no longer looking at him, or even at the gun in his hand. It was fixed instead upon a point above him. He tried to say *what the hell are you looking at*. His mouth moved, but his throat wouldn't work. The sound came out as a strangled rasp. There was something behind him. He slowly began to turn, even though he knew somehow that it was too late. Fate had shifted out of his favor.

Lucius turned, tilting his head upwards, where he beheld a great carapace rising out of the boiling mass of turtles. Neither Lucius nor Noah would have been able to put a name to it. It had come into being before the Earth had a moon in its sky, and had not been seen in living memory. Even the pictograms of its effigy had long since crumbled to dust. But the songs had persevered, passed down through the ages by holy men and women into the ears and hearts of their children.

The leviathan seemed to unfold itself as it heaved out of the riverbed. An orifice opened at the fore of the shell like a castle gate, bony plates grinding and tendons creaking as a monstrous, alien head pushed forth. The visage was as much snake as it was catfish or alligator, and yet it was none of these.

A lost memory surfaced, rising up from the deep waters of the minds of both men like the huge, encrusted shell of the creature emerging before them. Great-gran and her campfire tales - legends of giant, secretive things that inhabited the lost places of the world. They roamed lonely forests or misty mountain ranges. Others lay in deep, dark lakes. And some lived in rivers.

She'd sung to all of her children in a strange language that none of them knew but nonetheless understood, songs of magic and monsters - spirits who protected nature and the lands around their home. *Riverlings.* That's what she'd called them, and there was one that ruled them all - The Old Man of the River. Myth had been reborn before their eyes.

A swell of displaced water rocked the the craft and propelled it away, giving them full view of the enormity - and a terrible, surreal perspective of their own mortality.

Great, rank sheets of muck dropped from its misshapen bulk into the river, showering the men in the boat with clots of mud and debris. Feelers sprouted from around its maw, writhing in frenzy and snapping the air like whips. Thick tentacles sprung from the water and thrashed like downed power lines. Noah could see rows of suckers running along the bottoms, with hooked barbs in each that clicked and rattled as they convulsed. A deep rumble emanated from somewhere within the thing, making the water churn and bubble like potion in a cauldron. Other limbs began to surface around it, segmented and armored and ending in pincers that looked big enough to cut an elephant in half.

It was primordial, an experiment of Mother Nature, perhaps undertaken during Her adolescence when She was yet uncertain what was required of an elemental god. It seemed She'd ultimately decided that, as monsters went, bigger was better. *And this is the only God we'll ever know*, he thought distantly.

In his delirium, Noah had a vision of it lying in the silt bed of this same long-ago river. He imagined it clearly, rising from the murky water, open-mouthed and waiting, while human sacrifices were thrown, shrieking, from the muddy banks by raving fanatics who might have worshipped it.

Humans are at their most unpredictable under duress. Often, an individual is blissfully unaware of who they are until faced with a life-or-death situation. One will flee while another will choose to fight. Others freeze, dying in place at the whim of an active shooter. Noah should have been terrified, and he knew it - but instead found himself humbled to be in the presence of this creature. He was suddenly overcome with emotion, and his eyes swelled with tears. He wanted to articulate this in some way to his cousin, but he would never get the chance.

Cousins Noah and Lucius were opposites in many ways, but never so starkly as at this crossroads in reality. Noah had managed to sit up but could only stare in wonder.

Lucius was experiencing terror at a level he'd never known or even imagined was possible. Not even the prospect the of mass extermination of his species had ever stirred such visceral fear. He had a brief, irrational thought that the monster had somehow been awakened by the the sludge he'd poured into the river. Then it roared.

It was a sound that strummed the very chords of his mortality, but even in the grip of the waking nightmare in which he found himself, he did what came naturally. Lucius raised his Kimber 1911 and began firing as fast as humanly possible. He was still pulling the trigger long after his magazine emptied.

The Lazarus reappears, drifting silently from the dark to beach upon the slick, muddy bank. It hushes the bullfrogs and other wary critters singing in the lattice of reeds. For awhile the silence is broken only by the soft lapping of water against the hull. Once they feel safe – an interval of time known only to critters – they resume their courtship songs.

Noah gets his legs beneath him and carefully steps ashore, falling twice before finding solid ground. By the time he thinks to look back, the current has caught the Lazarus and drawn it away. He doesn't watch it go. It will never be seen again, and soon it will be as though it never existed. Lazarus was not registered to any Lucius Strahan. Neither were the trailer or the F-350 that brought them to the middle of nowhere. They are somewhere far away upstream, already beginning to sink into the marshy earth. They river will claim all before any is discovered, just as it has taken their now-departed owner. Noah will not think about them ever again.

The fog in his head is slowly clearing, revealing flashes of the otherworldly events just behind him.

Noah looking down the barrel of a pistol, large as the bore of a cannon.

Sharp clicking of Lucius dry firing.

The gargantuan, serrated claw which had swept across the deck and severed Lucius at the waist.

The bulk of a river god receding and the hush of the world resettling in its wake.

All but one of these visions will soon disappear, and the one that remains will only manifest in the deepest of dreams. In it, Noah stands alone at the bow of a ruined boat, nose to nose with a massive, misshapen head. It is so close that he can see his reflection on the slick surface of a great, black eye. It smells of humid jungle and river mud, old stone and lost religions. It is ethereal as all dreams are – an interval of vague and unaccountable time – although Noah understands each time that he has been judged and found worthy.

The stars are wide awake and casting their shimmer Earthward. By their light, Noah soon finds a remote firebreak and follows it towards the distant highway. Though the winding water fades quickly from sight, her song accompanies him for a long while. It will never completely leave him, like a whisper of things both real and imagined.

There is no sight or sound of traffic for a long while, but he will get there by and by. When he does, someone will see to it that he makes it home. This is river country. It is home to people – and other things – that know their own. He was Of The River, and of the lands surrounding it and into which it breathed life.

Four months later.

"Frankly Mister Strahan, I can't imagine how we, or anybody else for that matter, could possibly have overlooked your existence for so long."

Those were the words, verbatim, that Gerald Carroway had spoken to Noah. The man was CEO of Tether Corporation, the first billionaire that Noah had ever met, and he was still coming to terms with his new situation.

He hadn't submitted a resumé to Tether, or any other large corporation for that matter, so it had come as quite the surprise to have been offered a position. That offer had come in person. He'd been sitting in Jackson's when the delegation entered. They'd been dressed casually enough but had nonetheless drawn the marked attention that all strangers do in small towns. Doris - third of her name to work the grills and registers - noticed them first. She'd raised her bright red eyebrows and given a "hmph" of surprise, causing every head in the place to turn.

They'd had an official air about them, but lacked the hawk-eyed intensity of law enforcement which might have gotten Noah's guard up. No sheriffs had been to see him, and nobody in his family had asked about Lucius more than once or twice following Noah's return from the river. They knew that the pair had gone out together to fish. Noah just said they'd talked about another of Lucius' business schemes, that he hadn't been interested, and they'd gone their separate ways.

It wasn't unlike his cousin to disappear on "business" for weeks or even months. Noah understood that if someone ever came across Luc's truck, he might find himself talking to authorities, but other than that brief consideration he hadn't thought about Lucius at all.

But the Tether folks' easy manner had put Noah immediately at ease. They'd been as down to earth as if they were locals... but there were stark differences in their demeanor that became quickly apparent. They had extraordinarily thoughtful and optimistic views of how the world should operate, almost all of which mirrored Noah's own. In the course of an hour, he was packed and on his way to the airport, where a private plane had whisked them all away to Tether headquarters in Montana.

The interview itself seemed a formality. Carroway did most of the talking, describing in great detail Tether's vision for the future. Noah had accepted, of course. After only five minutes in Gerry's office, there was never a question that he wouldn't do so. It wasn't the salary that had left him breathless and made him sag in his chair, but more so the opportunity that Tether offered.

Tether had a small, select inner circle of people, Gerry had said... a Council of sorts. They were working on a project, and that it was unprecedented. It was something that people like Noah were ideally suited for, and that he wouldn't want to miss out on for all the world. It was precisely the kind of thing Noah had always dreamed of.

And now here he was, packing his things for the move to Montana and a new beginning. He paused, looking out the window at the beautiful summer day. *What would he do, to change things?* He mused. He closed his suitcase with a click that echoed through the empty rooms of the apartment he would never seen again.

If he were being candid with himself, given what he'd so recently learned from Lucius about the unbelievable depths of greed, Noah believed he would do just about anything to change the world for the better. Just like his departed cousin... he might even kill for that.

TWO
THE SHADOWS KNOW

Foreverwhere. Oasis in the desert of my mind. I spend as much time here as I dare, and then some. I've taken to pressing my luck more and more, going well beyond the edges of my intent, perhaps too far for my own good. But this is the only place where I know true peace, and who could be blamed for wanting more of a good thing?

Would that I could remain, but Otherwhere - the real world - calls like a lost child. It holds to me like the thin, gossamer anchor web of a marauding spider, an invisible leash with unyielding tensile strength. Rules, in general, mean little to me, but returning to Otherwhere is one of the few I must obey. And I'd be lying to myself if I said I didn't enjoy my time there. What agent of chaos does not enjoy any opportunity to create havoc?

Chaos is my essence and purpose, and I am glad of it. It is the only dependable constant, the flowing river of reality. I am fortunate to be among those rare things born to navigate its treacherous currents. All monsters thrive in chaos, but time must be spent apart - if only to provide perspective. I know this as all alchemists do. Humanity is an amalgam, and those who do not create potions are merely ingredients to be used by others. I only appear to blend in, but it's like the subtle blur of alcohol in water. Those who notice and think to look more closely quickly discover that I do not mix well.

I was not cut from the threadbare cloth that stitches humankind together like a desiccated funeral shroud. I will never stoop to ooze about like a slug, waiting for the crushing weight of disappointment. No indeed. I'm a biter, a stinger; deceptively beautiful and brutally armored. At the core, I am a thing of purpose, but even things crave freedom from the constraints of time and the tedious dead weight of the human condition. I paint myself upon this canvas of Foreverwhere like a synesthete's fever dream. Shall I render a field of screams in broad strokes of violent red?

A creation of sheer willpower, Foreverwhere is mine, at least inasmuch as anything can be owned. I am closer to paradise here than most will ever know, and it's probably more than I deserve. I come and go as I please, and it's never the same. This subtle flux makes it near perfect, although I've ensured there are no dead vistas or sudden drops into darkness to avoid. There are plenty of both in the Otherwhere.

Here We roam untethered, but carefully nonetheless. One can never know what might have become lodged in the sulci of the mindscape. I'm not afraid, mind you. I don't deal in fear; it is a clumsy and expensive emotion. Caution, however, is always priceless. I'd never have come so far if I weren't cognizant of the worlds around me. There is no shame in taking care. Not even gods are ever entirely safe, especially not in their own minds.

TETHERED

The pull of the Otherwhere is becoming uncomfortable. For a moment, I'm tempted to ignore it. Perhaps one day I will, just to see what happens – but not today. So I turn away from the vast expanse of my stray thoughts and set out briskly upon the path of inevitability.

Foreverwhere is a personification of dark beauty, and the Mourning Garden is its heart. It's no mystery why I choose it to be the first thing I see upon arrival and the last before I go. It is a work in progress, full of misbegotten ways, but all paths eventually lead here. There is a sense of something tearing as I enter. It's a feeling that I do not recognize yet seems somehow familiar.

I trail my fingertips across the cold wards of the garden's boundary, bleached white and worn beyond memory. The Quintessences envelop me as soon as I cross over. Their loathing coats me, invigorating and unexpected as the sudden frost that kills flowers under a pale midsummer moon. Each had a name, once upon a time. Some were known to me, but I don't think on it. Maybe the lichens that enshroud them and their mementos could care. Certainly there must be some in the Otherwhere who still remember them, friends and relatives who visit their plots with diminishing frequency, leaving flowers to wilt at the feet of their cold stone monuments, and tokens that will be casually stolen by greedy passersby.

It is said that we all die twice. The first is when the mind sparks its last thought and the heart goes cold and grey. The second is the last time someone speaks our name. It is of little consequence to me. Like roses by any name, people must all wither and die. Still, they make a lovely compost for my garden.

Tendrils of mist play at my feet, like blind, amorphous snakes in the clover. Many seeds have I sown here in my short time. Those that bear fruit and flower peer up kaleidoscopically. I pick a crimson, my favorite color. It verily drips red, desperate to feel again... if only for a moment. Dew beads and trickles down my bare legs, tributaries in miniature that meld into rivers, torrents rushing down smooth flesh finally to cascade over cliffs between my toes. This happens and does not happen. It is a thing of the mind; the only reality that matters. Skeletal fingers of heat lightning reach across the firmament, and the death rattle of thunder that follows rouses the Something.

I've known of it since before I was born, the Something. It resides in the dark oubliette of my subconscious. There it waits, like a rusty animal trap, the moist chunks of its secret thoughts churning like fresh chum in the wake of our inspired machinations. Now animated, It grates like stones at work in a dry gizzard.

I do not know precisely what It is, but a conundrum of which I am constantly aware. All I know for sure is that It must be fed. That is critically important information for anyone inhabited by a ravenous parasitic twin - especially if that twin is not human. The Something is the only thing in all of creation of which I am wary. Exhilarating for me, really, the subtle relentlessness of It constantly pressing and looking for voids in the wall that separates us. We should all be so lucky to be fascinated by the dangerous mystery of our unknowable selves. How, I wonder, does It regard me? Only our shadows can know. It brings to mind an old tune, fit for an old soul.

Me... And, My, ShaaaaAAAaaaadow.

It is a dark thing that does not fade even in the brightest, most hopeful light - tangible in a way that is difficult to describe, and bound to me more surely than any shadow could. I understood early on that it was making me strong, and far more vital than anyone of my petite stature could possibly be - like living armor grown beneath my skin.

Even the most unimaginative and stoic of holy men might be tempted to pronounce me possessed, but they'd be wrong. No host would collaborate with a demon as willingly as I've come to do with the Something.

But it's no partnership. We share, but grudgingly. It would kill me if It could live without me, I'm sure. And up to now, I'm only assuming that It cannot. Not yet, anyway. Likewise, it has always been my plan to coexist quietly, bide my time, and then drain the Something of everything It has to give. I did try. Once. It didn't work out well for either of us. Not at all.

I wasn't surprised at the outcome and, in truth, I wouldn't want it to be easy. No participation trophies for killers, as it were. Effortless victory is disappointing, and should be. Nothing of real value has ever been gained through peaceful effort or compromise. They are the brittle tools of the weak. Growth and progress are only begotten by the persistence of unreasonable people - and whatever levels of violence are necessary and appropriate to the ends. Even at my comparatively tender age, I've come to believe that anyone who says differently is probably selling something.

For now, things are as they are and must be. I don't concern myself, especially not here in the soft, ethereal light of my Foreverwhere. Wasting worry upon what is beyond one's control is the purest form of madness. Disaster visits everyone. Dread only ensures that you suffer twice.

The Something and I understand one another as much as we need to. We are creators, harbingers of mayhem, and only together can We deliver it with the intensity it deserves. It's all that matters, and We do it so very well, though it is peculiar that We can never occupy the same space. It's as though this human carcass is but a studio, a mobile workshop of sloshing organs and bones bound in hide. We are artists, voyeurs who, in turn, wipe the foggy panes of bleary stained glass and behold the tableau of Our collaborations. At work, It is the armature, and I the dark matter that fleshes it. The Something is no poet, but the deep green hiss of the garden is thick in my ears and inspires a verse.

Neither sinister or dexter may clap alone, but together snap like breaking bone.

The path is jigged and jagged with icy streams that pulse like blue-black veins. Scarcely ankle-deep, they take the breath away, just like Us. The waters collect in small, restless pools that contain submerged cameos of recent work. Here is a visage, just beneath the surface, frozen in its last moment – blotchy and mottled in descending shades of petechial pale. Silly thing to pretend it's still alive. I nudge it back into the eddies with an indifferent toe, and the Something shifts again, slowly uncoiling and snuffling with interest. I imagine a shiny, emerald sliver of dragon's eye smoldering, ever watchful. Restless. It's a greedy thing. You'd find Its like in a razed field, clinging to the damp bottom of an old stone slab, waiting for some curious fool to slide their fingers under.

"No rest for the wicked," I say aloud as We cross the bridge of broken dreams and pass into the garden proper. Below, the stream widens in welcome. Its bed is lined with even older tributes. Empty sockets stare up sightlessly, hopeless pits sunken in algae-slick bone. Beards of water grass wave in the melancholy current. I can smile a genuine smile here, and I do; at the fecund black soil, the clouds pregnant with their infant storms, and the trees of perpetual Indian Summer. The sun kisses my face.

Even monsters can appreciate beauty, and some can even make art with finesse worthy of the masters. One might even consider that monsters pursue desire with a single-minded dedication that few could maintain or even understand. We are born to it in the way of the bee - servants of a higher purpose. Our course is unique. Transcendent. The road of the artist has rarely been smooth, and I wouldn't change that for anything. Could I ever forgive myself for not seeing it through?

I draw in a deep, damp breath and wish the air could be as sweet and guileless as in the Otherwhere. Bokeh lights dance for me, and it makes me think how joyous it would be to share the beauty. Is there a special someone out there waiting even now, a soul who would love the peculiar light of my world? Might they even come to appreciate the twisted shadows that grow when that illumination wanes? Don't be afraid, I'd whisper; nothing hunts me here. Could another ever love me? Would their touch caress my soul like a sunset, skin clean and smelling of new rain? Would the Something be jealous? Could It be? Three makes a crowd, or so it's said.

As if in answer, It shifts inside me again like a phantom limb. It is persistent as a splintered thought that now and then breaks the skin but lodged so firmly in the bone that it can never be pulled free.

I exhumed the Something on my seventh birthday. The world had been a promised adventure. I was coming into my own, just glimpsing the potential of who I might one day become. But several somethings happened on that day that would change me forever.

I'd grown up believing, as children do, the things I'd been taught. What can a child do, after all, but to grow as sown? And what is to come of it? How can anything become other than twisted when the soil is a bed of lies? So. Many. Lies. There was pain, confusion, and despair. Then, in the midst of my inability to come to terms with what had been done to me, the Something awoke. It would be the best birthday present I would ever receive.

But living with the Something is a challenge in itself. It's like playing chess with a hateful machine, its razor-sharp moving parts spinning at blurring speed, waiting for a wrong move. Checkmated, I would be macerated into red, bite-sized chunks. But I've proved stronger than I could have known, made keen and sure as a whetted edge by this endless game of cat and mouse. Irony in this, for the Something Itself sharpens the very weapon that keeps It at bay.

The air is saturated with lilting insectile harmonies and the percussion of frogs. Black butterfly, so brave to light upon my shoulder. I allow this. Nothing happens here but by My will. Here, I am Tolerance - I am ALL. This deep in the very heart of the garden, not even the infernal buzzing undertone of the Otherwhere can reach me.

Typically, only the hopelessly insane know the sound. It is dissonance of the worst imaginings, like clots of sonic venom swirling in the ear canals; babies shrieking in hunger, the agonized cries of burning animals, the harsh gurgle of slow strangulation. It is the desperate clawing of the prematurely interred.

To be rid of it, I once pierced my eardrums with a long finishing nail I found in father's toolbox - which accomplished nothing except to draw unwanted attention. It was before I accepted Us, and learned to draw strength from it. We are more careful now, although I wonder if Mr. And Mrs. Kadverian knew what they wrought when they conceived me. My parents, with their schemes and experiments and Tether's greater good at the center of their every thought and deed. Did they take into consideration that they were building better than they intended? I suppose the more pertinent question is: if they knew what We've become, would they change anything? It's said that the apple doesn't fall far from the tree. I don't care about that, except to wonder how far it rolls.

The garden has lulled me, as it often does, and I've drifted. Would my special someone see the sudden distance in my expression, poke me playfully; smile and tell me that I am in my own little world? I could only smile in return. Based on what I know of the true nature of the wider world, I would consider it a compliment.

The echo of a scream slices into my thoughts and freezes me in my tracks. It shouldn't be possible – but I knew I was pressing my luck. And I suppose that even the strongest minds wander.

I am a singularity, deliberately gifted with, among other things, pure hyperthymesia. I recall the white electric spark of coming into existence, splitting, the reddish liquid comfort of the womb, and the traumatic constriction of birth. I was aware of my first agonized breath and, in the exact moment, understood that there would one day be a last. It is no wonder that so many fail to adjust to the violent recycling of consciousness. The soul becomes attached to the flesh far too easily.

As if reading my mind, a shepherd of souls appears. It happens like an explosion in reverse – a coalescing dream of flame and sound. But as it takes form and I see what it's becoming, I can't help but laugh aloud. A unicorn. Of all things. He could have chosen any form, but it is fitting.

He is an Emulai, the opposite of a shadow. How very exquisite he is, how beautiful. I can only imagine what We look like to him.

Emulai are passion incarnate, beings of hard polychromatic energy. This one has to be ancient... and inconceivably powerful. Most aren't significant enough to disturb the edges of my outermost thoughts, much less manage corporeal manifestation. To dare challenge me – especially here – his essence must verge on primordial. Flashing like a Humboldt at hunt, the heat of his fury is severe as a forge fire of the old gods. He is the epitome of white magic, snorting flame and ripping at the caliginous walls of my domain.

We are as opposed as enemies must be, but I do not hate him. I understand the fae, and with understanding comes acceptance. And respect? Definitely. Anything brave enough to act according to its true nature deserves at least that. It's not reciprocated, I'm sorry to say, and more's the pity. There is much we could learn from one another. What keeps us from ever finding common ground is the notion that I would destroy him – or any of his kind – if the opportunity presented. They're not wrong, of course. Never misunderstand. Emulai know us for what we are as well. He is barely more than a suggestion, an equine cloud that seems solid enough to touch, but I have a sense of how it would feel to flay him. Would that I were capable of such a thing alone.

Were we to ever find ourselves together in the Otherwhere, I would happily share my valuable time over coffee or perhaps a glass of some amusing house wine. The conversation would be one to cherish. Then would come the sheer bliss of rending him, pulling his spine and sucking the marrow from his shattered bones while all around people shrieked and scrambled. Blood would spurt and rain down on the china shattering on the sidewalk – perhaps with a tinkling of silverware as an accompaniment.

Destroying an Emulai's shell would be entertaining but ultimately futile. The entity within is immortal and would immediately find another body to inhabit. More importantly, only a being with a whole, uncompromised soul can destroy Emulai. For Us, it would necessitate a relinquishing of Our separate identities. I'm not confident that We would be strong enough to kill it, honestly, but the effort of destroying such a powerful faery creature would most assuredly leave me weakened. There is no doubt in my mind that the Something would take the opportunity to assume control of this body. There is also the possibility that it would kill Us both; unless of course the Something, like an Emulai, is also immortal... which would go a long way in explaining Its reckless enthusiasm for carnage.

I'm not sure how I know some of the things I know. It's not the type of knowledge that's written down. It's enough that I do know them, instinctively and well, the same way a young snake knows to inject all of its venom every time it bites.

What We are must be rare indeed. I've yet to meet another and, as far as I know, there is no name for it. The term "Monster" seems like an oversimplification of taxonomy. Still, one must consider that those unfortunate enough to meet things like Us are not likely to survive such an encounter. So, unless the authorities get lucky enough to capture and study one of us, I suppose monster will have to do.

If I could find another like me, however, hunting fae would become a different game entirely. Two monsters, playing nice and working to the same end, would tear through Emulai like a Kansas tornado. And there are others out there. I sense them sometimes, and best when the Something is restless. There is an unpleasant electric tingle when monsters are nearby. At times, I have been close enough to touch. Intuition suggests that I keep my distance whenever it happens. Nothing is more dangerous to any monster than one of its own kind.

As for the uninvited unicorn in my garden, he won't last much longer no matter how strong he is, and when he goes it will be as though he never existed. We can't sense the auras of Emulai in the Otherwhere. I might have passed this very creature on a busy street. He may be one of my teachers, or a neighbor, or live in a grass hut in Africa. It's even possible that he - or she - has yet to be born.

However, just like with others of my kind, physical contact strips away the facade. I am always covertly touching strangers hoping that chance will smile on me one day and reveal a child of magic.

What a specimen this one is. His human counterpart must surely be special. His heart is thunder, and the sudden desire to know it nearly tears me from the sanctity of the garden. Sadly, bravado is all he has here, and I need do no more than smile to cause him pain. He roars flame, tosses his head, and strikes the earth; sparks of white fire fly from between the delicate cloven hooves. Ah, such spirit! I so hope we meet someday in the flesh.

I clench the clover between my toes and approach. He blazes in a strident flare of grudging retreat; for a breath, he is as mighty as a supernova. Then he is compelled to go from this hallowed place. He bellows in rage and a last tongue of flame erupts from his mouth and turns the ground before him into glass. I can feel the heat even from this side of the veil. It is an impressive display, but rules are rules. He sparks, finally, and sizzles into nothing, and I swallow what's left of the spent emotion. He's done some damage, though. A hint of rough buzzing finds me somehow, rubs me wrong. I have stayed too long.

The sound of clear water playing beckons from a primal fount; prisms on a curtain of silvery spray await Us. I have long and lovingly cultivated this, the heart of my garden, and it bears me treasures.

Berries bend the slender branches of the hedges that ring Us; swollen bulbs of crimson peek from amidst leaves the color and texture of a midsummer tan. A limb recoils as I reach for it, and the entire bush shudders when I pluck the fruit. Warmth runs down my chin, staining my lips and fingers. I have adorned the verge with trophies; pretty ribbons and bangles dangling here and there - curios, watches, and rings that weigh the branches and make them bounce with adolescent firmness. A tremor shakes me, a final reminder that I am needed elsewhere.

I leave the hedge to its misery and part the haze, revealing the portal- the dark pool that hides the gateway to the world. I slip in like a baptism, sighing along with the waterfalls as they hiss in pleasure and pain. See there, just above the surface, the pretty blue eyes of the pigtailed crocodile? Chilled water flows into my open and waiting mouth, dousing the smoldering grin.

Finally, I release and plummet. It catches me by surprise each and every time, a rush of excitement that offsets the agitation of my departure from the gardens. The Something senses it too, and there's a shared anticipation of what's to come.

We touch down gently and open Our eyes to find that my body has been appropriately and splashingly busy in my absence. We stand quite still, chin in hand, regarding a twilit lane of dark cobbles and the stately home at its end, as a master chef might an egg from some exotic creature. How might it be prepared, once cracked?

The inconvenient obstacle of security is no more, but there is little to be gained by hurrying things now. It's unseemly, plus, unlike most chefs, I run a risk of becoming the meal and must give every endeavor due patience. The Something and I sway in the breeze like herons hunting lizards in the cattails, invisible in all the ways that matter, floating toward the house – our blank canvas. I feel the fire of foreboding stoked, not unlike the right kind of touch in just the right place. The Something uncoils all the way, and I turn, thinking that one of these times I might see it trailing behind me like the black tail of some nightmarish kite. Instead, there are only shadows thrown by the dancing flames of gas lamps that light the drive. They fret like ghosts at Our approach, wishing they could scream a warning to the living.

There are doorways, and then there are doorways. We pass through most thoughtlessly for they are but simple passages. Others are thresholds which, once crossed, offer no hope of returning. I have passed through more of the latter than most ever will. No two are ever the same, while others prove one of a kind. Going in is delightful in a manner of which I will never tire. So much potential, each and every time. In this, absolute recollection is a gift like none other. In the catacombs of my mind there are no simple, sad flashes of memory easily lost, or worse, fade like precious watercolor paintings in the sun. I am whenever and whenever I wish to be. I bob in the swirling waters of the Foreverwhere even as I walk the labyrinthine halls of my memory. And I am here, on this night, fidgeting anxiously before yet another doorway.

I know this place. I have been carried through its splendor, kissed, cuddled, and fussed over by those inside before I could even walk on my own. It was years ago, but it's as if I were only just here.

Though We are here with purpose, I admire these people who would choose to dwell within art, and I wonder if they would appreciate that if they knew.

The door is a massive thing, formed of redwood that was milled before electricity was discovered. It is as formidable as a castle gate. It has been recently refinished, and the warm amber scent of freshly sanded wood and varnish hangs like oiled flowers. I place both palms upon it and feel it in its entirety.

The house it wards is a handsome masterpiece of architectural inspiration. It must have been a labor of love for the long-dead craftsmen who shaped and breathed life into it - the dust of their souls embedded in the mortar, the cut nails that bind the hand-planed timber dipped into their heart's blood. I close my eyes and see their ghosts, summer sweat running down their arms, the song of the hammer and chisel echoing afar. No simpleminded, cheap day laborers so common today, they created because they'd had no choice. It was their nature. We who discover and embrace our purpose are the most fortunate of creatures. Might some of the tools have passed into the eager hands of descendants, I wonder, and did the magic follow?

The last of the summer crickets chirp in the air as I take it all in. I almost leave, for this is not personal. It wouldn't be the first time I've done so. To create, I must alter this place forever. There will always be other venues. Occasionally, the muse fails us all.

But not tonight. It is upon me and I must express myself. When they speak of me as an artist, and speak they shall, it will be to marvel at the ritual and mystery of every canvas.

The ring of sticky keys turns my pocket inside out, and I tussle to tuck it back in. The security guard had more keys than a high school janitor. You would think that someone so wed to the old ways would be wiser... and a lot more careful.

You expect carelessness from the young, inexperienced as most of them are to evil. Children of all ages fall prey to it every day. Kittens and puppies, you say? Why yes, I'd love to climb into your primer and rust-colored van with the tinted windows, friendly stranger! Do you also have candy?

But the guard was old enough to know better. He suspected that something was off with me. I saw that clear as day in his eyes. He simply couldn't or wouldn't acknowledge the danger, and became a twitching, bleeding testament to ineptitude - the rough sketch and color study, as it were, which precede so many great works.

The herd has grown deaf to the frantic screaming of dire warning. They become softer with each passing generation, fascinated by the technology that enslaves them. Bless their little hearts. The things they come to depend upon fail them so quickly. The Lord of this manor is wealthy and complacent in equal measure, a lesson that ... aaaaah yes, the tumblers roll with a soft, metallic crunch like the cocking of a well-maintained pistol. It took less time to find the right key than it did to kill the alarm system. A costly oversight, but it wouldn't have mattered in the end. If We want in, there is no keeping Us out. If it must occasionally become a noisy affair, then so be it.

This time around, at least, technology disappoints. It is the newest religion - and mightiest of all. Its followers are unique in that they do not fear it. They regard it with only the proper amount of awe, for it is logical, orderly, and purer than any that have come before. Let us prey.

There are no splinters in the oak floors to snag on my socks, and I am not heavy enough to make the joists tattle on me. In the gymnasium-sized great room there isn't a single irresponsibly burning electric light to betray me. It's only an observation, mind you. I don't judge. I never really knew these people, snuggled up above and dreaming in the warmth of their beds. They could be the best or worst sort. They've never wronged me. I don't know if they have wronged others, though it's likely. I might come to find those things out eventually, or not. I don't care. Do you understand? Can you?

My hand skitters up the mahogany banister like a pale spider, pausing at the top where a skewed panel of pale bluish light wavers on the wall across from the doorway of the master suite. The Something is awake now, enormous within me, and I marvel anew that others don't see It - never sense Our approach.

Now. Should I begin here with the two large humps spooning beneath the goose-down? The ceiling fan ruffles a tuft of his exposed salt-and-pepper. She is snoring very softly. I drum my fingers on the door jamb as I consider, lips pursed in the gloom. No. Better to start small, I think.

Marching up and down the hall in nursery rhyme cadence, eenie-meenie-miney-moe, into which room shall We go?

The first life flutters in my hands like a baby bird and we sigh together. The Something writhes like a downed power line and must soon be given Its turn. In the hallway again, moving quickly, Our progress is now marked by a dark, smeary footprint that will soak into the wood and never completely leave. It might be premature, but We take the time to sign this most recent addition to Our great work, a handprint upon the embossed leather wallpaper that looks black in the dark. It is a somewhat larger mark than those on the very earliest of my pieces, the amusing finger paintings that used to adorn the refrigerator.

When compared, this autograph will not match the other children's prints, leaving no doubt about who came to call. How the detectives must puzzle over this mysterious growing personalization that began appearing in random homes many years ago.

On to the next, then. It has been some time since my last visit, and the Lord and Lady of the Manor have been prolific. Making Our way down the hall, We visit two more rooms. More berries and shiny things for my garden. I can almost taste them.

His Lordship suddenly stumbles heavily into the hall, finally jolted awake by the immense wrong that has come to call. He is a huge man, seeming even more so backlit and featureless. His silhouette's head is cocked to the side in confusion as he advances, belting a robe. It is me that he sees, not Us. There is a clumsy moment when his bare foot slips in a slick wetness that should not be. The shape of him pauses, lifts its foot. Too late, it dawns on him, and he becomes still as stone as it settles in. I regard him for a heartbeat. I could do it alone. I'm so much stronger than I look. But the Something was made for this sort of encounters, and it's his turn anyway.

An antique hallway table explodes beneath Our weight, expensive shards digging into skin and hide as the three of us thrash about. The man has just enough time to rasp a little girl's name. I am not your precious daughter, Milord. The

Lady appears then, screams, and makes the acquaintance of the Something. Through it all I feel like a maestra conducting her orchestra of spiked, bloody instruments.

It is over almost too quickly, but I try to never dwell in disappointment. One must enjoy a blessed, well-earned silence. The Something should be sated, and I am thinking that it will rest when I realize that We have left a room unexplored. Silly of me, but in the heat of the moment, even I have half-human flaws. The occupants of the other rooms were boys, and so it must be the little girl, the Lord's Last Word, who remains.

In her room, the small, freshly-peeled bed is empty, but the lacy pillow is still warm with her body heat. Her little nightlight is on - small children know enough to be appropriately afraid of the dark. Odd that I do not feel her fear. She has either fled or hidden. Probably hiding. Searching the gloom through half-lidded eyes, I hope for the latter. I do love a game of hide and seek.

In the hallway again, looking about, We hear a soft jangling. At the far end, a shape slides around the corner. Is it Our little mystery friend, come back to see if it's safe? No. Not even close. It is, instead, one of the largest dogs I have ever seen. I can't make out the breed in the questionable light, but it looks to be more monster than animal.

The moon watches over all, Her sublimelight accentuating the vibrancy of the stipples and splashes upon the walls and floor. The dog creeps towards Us, hackles raised like the spines of a boar, and a frisson of anticipation raises the fine hairs on my arms.

It's not quite close enough for Us to spring when it suddenly stops, freezing in a shaft of bluish-white light. It is a beast of an animal, a veritable song of strength and beauty, and all Ours. I've always been a dog person, I think with a grin. It huffs a challenge that I feel in the soles of my feet, eyes twinkling balefully as it crouches, poised to do what instinct compels. Just like Us. A rumble from its throat rolls down the hall and makes me shiver despite the heat of my own blood. The Something stirs again, but I have no want or need of it.

Dogs are like Emulai in their way. Human or monster, they seem to sense what We are, and I delight whenever I encounter them. Diluted breeds flee sometimes, screeching in terror, but the pure descendants of the wolves do not know fear. In its place is a fighting spirit and single-minded ferocity which no human could hope to match.

It edges forward another step. Then another. Yes, beautiful one, come to me, whatever you are. Too small to be a Malinois. It is big enough to be a Shepherd or Rottweiler, but either would have already attacked. I take a step towards it, and the Something surges like a marlin, a distraction which I must work to ignore. But why does my lovely watchdog not attack?

I think of the girl-child, somewhere in the scary, uncertain dark, little hands over her ears and eyes screwed tightly shut. Wherever she is, she will wait for the time this will take. At this moment, the dog is very much the priority. Very well, I tell it silently, I will come to you.

The massive canine tenses and crouches lower as I start to pad closer, the moist tip-splotch-tap-splotch of my feet sounding loud against the silence of the high hall. It is my own growl now that rumbles in my chest. The dog's eyes flicker, twin coals in the darkness. Then, inexplicably, it abruptly rises, cocking its shaggy head as though someone were crinkling a bag of treats. The Something suddenly rages in me, finally capsizing my concentration. Could the timing be worse? Honestly, there is no satisfying some Things. By the time I force It down, the dog is gone. The ticking of its claws retreating into the dark drags my face into a scowl.

But this could work in Our favor, I think. The dog might very well lead us to the girl. The notion of having them both thrills me. It's encouraging, but before I can even think to take another step I feel a presence – right behind me. There is a soft, furtive noise, a rush of displaced air, and then something hard strikes the back of my skull. There is a sound that I feel as much as hear – KOONK! Stars explode behind my eyes and the floor rushes up to greet me.

When I wake, I remain purposefully still. I change nothing, not even the cadence of my breathing. I can't have been out for more than a few moments, and it's unlikely that my ambusher could begin to contemplate how resilient I am. A slight wiggle informs me, however, that I am also hogtied. I smile against the cool floorboards. It was deftly done, I have to admit.

She did it exactly the way I had to before I was strong enough. A smaller person must always use a weapon of some sort and strike with just enough force to incapacitate without causing too much damage. Larger, stronger prey has to be secured as soon as possible so that it cannot fight back, and can thereby be enjoyed at leisure.

Doing this type of thing well takes a bit of practice. It's easier to crush a skull than one might think.

Another wiggle confirms that I am trussed quite snugly. I haven't been gagged, however, and why bother? Only the dead are within earshot, and it's been my experience that they never mind a little more noise.

Tiny hands, stronger than they should be, grip my shoulder and turn me onto my side. Little footsteps move away, and after a moment, warm light swells in the hallway. The home is even more lovely in the soft, intimate glow of Tiffany wall sconces. The ceiling is higher from my unanticipated vantage, sculpted and punctuated with a few large, rectangular baroque mirrors - just enough for it not to be tacky. There is one directly above, and the familiar visage of a young woman looks down upon Us. She is lithe and a little pale, with alarming blue eyes and a shock of thick auburn hair, which has been pulled back into a tight ponytail ... otherwise, it tends to get in the way. Getting caught up in one's own hair in the middle of things is inconvenient, I can tell you. It's impossible to know how old the Something is, but my image in the mirror on high is that of a fourteen-year-old girl, just turned the corner into womanhood. She manages a smirk at her predicament.

In this scenario, most humans would be terrified, secured thus and awaiting the inevitable - but not I. And certainly not Us. My reflection, the Something, and I are simply curious, and maybe a little embarrassed. It goes without saying that We are also definitely impressed.

The patter of little feet returns and she reappears, leaning into my field of vision and obscuring the Me in the mirror. She leans down and plants a small kiss on my forehead. It sends a violent, electric jolt thrilling throughout my body. It's a familiar feeling - but more acute than anything I've ever experienced. There can be no doubt what she is. The monster's touch is magic.

I might have known.

"Maddie," I say. It was the Lord's last word, and it belongs to her. Maddie is maybe six, but her cherubic face is overshadowed by an experience and cunning that should not be.

The dog lumbers up now, and joins her in the light, and the mystery of its breeding is answered. Cane Corso... possibly bred with a grizzly. Even on his haunches, he is still taller than she, their heads amusingly cocked in identical curiosity.

My limbs grow numb as she looms, more dangerous to me than any number of Lilliputians from this Gulliverious perspective, considering me with furrowed brow and the buds of her pursed cupid lips. She turns and ghosts away, stopping to peer long into each room. The dog never takes its eyes off me. Good boy. A plop of drool splats to the floor. He is her version of the Something, only occupying another shell. Her familiar.

When Maddie returns I see that she has dropped her mask. We all wear them, human and monster alike, though it would be hard to say who needs them most. Ugly truths need to be hidden, especially from those closest to us. She bends and dabs at a spot of thickening blood on my cheek, rubs it between her fingers, tastes it.

"Who are you?" The gravelly timbre of the witch grinds the question in her throat, just a hint, deep and discordant, almost unnoticeable beneath the sweet tinkling bell of her child's voice.

"An artist."

"Artist." She repeats tonelessly.

In her hand is a boning knife. Titanium would be my guess, given the sheen. Japanese characters etched into the blade.

Expensive. She taps it against her leg as she gazes about, patiently taking in the various spatterings of my work.

"Those were mine," she finally says, the words as cold and dispassionate as the blade in her hand. There is emotion in her voice, but it's not sadness. She doesn't grieve, and will never miss them. She's just disappointed.

"Yes," I reply with clinical flatness. It's an acknowledgment, not an apology. I wouldn't ever apologize, but I do empathize. How she must have cultivated them, waiting, just as I do with mine own. For creatures like us, patience isn't a virtue; instead, it is more of a dry marinade. I can picture her watching them day after day, busy with the various empty tasks with which they occupied themselves while unknowingly waiting to be butchered. Like me, she'd dreamed of that perfect night when she would have been the one to walk these halls with dark intent.

An undersized aluminum baseball bat lies beside me on the fine wool carpet runner. I wonder how long she watched through the crack in her door, like a trapdoor spider in pink pajamas. Just until I was distracted enough, and not a second more. She waited until I got a step too far ahead of myself, then tiptoed up and hit me.

We regard one another for what seems an eternity, and then she slowly bends towards Us. She has to set the knife down to turn me again, and the blade gives a twinkling, knowing wink. I have always preferred my subjects face up so I can watch their expressions, but to each their own. There are things I would like to have done, but I must confess that I've always wondered what it must be like to be on this end, raw material waiting to be transformed.

I feel a few tugs and wait for the pain. If a knife is appropriately sharp, a person won't know they've been cut until they see the blood. It can take a shockingly long time. Then there's a dull, burning ache that swells until it bursts like a frozen water pipe.

The air stirs as she moves away, and I wait for pain that doesn't come. Instead, I find that I can move my hands and feet. After a long moment, I start to turn. Slowly. Once I'm confident there won't be another swing of the bat, I sit up. She is still there, a few feet away, smartly just out of my reach. The knife in her hand remains bone dry, and now I look surprised in the flat mirror of the blade.

Well. Isn't this just something?

We are almost the same height in this position. She grins shyly, dainty fists balled precociously beneath her chin, but the smile does not touch her eyes. A cute little gap between her two front teeth makes her seem almost human, and I cannot help but smile back. Her familiar, his tag unimaginatively reading BEAST, gives me a good sniff and licks at the blood on my face.

What now? We could do what We do. She did well enough all by her lonesome, and no doubt would be even more formidable with her BEAST close by. But they'd have no chance if I let the Something back out. Probably not, anyway. I give them a long look. Regardless of how it might play out, I have a decision to make and ought to be quick about it. Do We make more art, or do We not? She's waiting, and the scales of the Something grind the seconds like mortar and pestle as He writhes. BEAST and the Something might get along. And they might not. A giggle gets away from me.

Inspired, I reach out and stroke her cheek, and whisper her name like a prayer. "Maddie."

Hadn't I always wanted a special someone? I think a little sister just might do. "My name is Rae," I say with a smile. With my index finger, I swab at a congealing puddle on the floor and give her a little red clown nose.

"Wanna help me find a unicorn?"

THREE
OFF THE MAP

Congratulations.

If you're reading this, you're either a credit to our species or extraordinarily lucky. In light of events that led to our current state, I'd guess the former. That kind of luck doesn't exist anymore. You'd have been consumed long before now.

I would digress as to how secure this place is, but you'll have already developed a good eye for that sort of thing. Take a load off and poke around. There are supplies and other useful things to be found if you look hard enough. We should always make use of good fortune whenever we have it.

It's a shame I couldn't be here to meet you, but I had a particularly good reason for not sticking around. There's no putting down roots anywhere in general anymore, but even staying in one spot for more than a few hours makes most people uneasy. And for good reason. You probably know what I mean.

There is no determinable period for restlessness to set in. Sometimes, you are just suddenly and unreasonably compelled to get the hell gone. You wake up from a dead sleep, holding your breath as you strain to hear over the sound of your thudding heartbeat and the moist click of your eyelids blinking in the dark. After a moment, you realize it wasn't a noise that roused you. Somewhere in the deepest recesses of your mind, where all the ancient, hard-wired instincts still live, an inner voice has whispered a warning. It is the descendant of voices that first suggested we make fires at the entrances to our caves to keep things out. You hear it when something wicked this way comes, and there's plenty out there - things constantly working out how to find and get at you. Given enough time, they will always find a way.

At best, we survivors only ever feel safe for a few days in one place, even in an armageddon-resistant bunker like this one. I've managed three days here. I'm betting you won't make it a week.

It's the toughest building I've ever been inside, but it's too quiet. It's difficult to think clearly without the ever-changing cacophony of the outside world flapping like old, dried-out skin. I can't even hear the steady rain that's been coming down for the last day and a half, even though it's been to my advantage.

Some of the sounds common to this new, wilder world of ours are horrible beyond description. Some seem as if they will never belong; all are preferable to a sudden dead silence. Nothing good comes of things whenever the environment grows unusually still, as it usually precedes noise of the worst sort. I've come to dread an absolute silence like the one that fills this place. It's like being buried alive.

TETHERED

Once one has grown accustomed to the otherworldly lullabies of things best left to the imagination, sleeping without them can be troublesome. There are mournful, caterwauling cries and deep, booming growls that vibrate the bones. Dreadful, hair-raising shrieks slice the quiet into wet, quivering chunks. The sonic landscape has been taken over by choirs of deadly fauna, but some of us have learned to dance to the dissonance.

Knowing your sounds can keep you alive. Even human screams are helpful, so long as they're not yours. Any scream of a particular pitch and volume informs us that someone is suddenly having their worst day. It's a sound that seems like it could not possibly come from human vocal cords, but there's no question it is.

Not long ago, we had the luxury of ignoring cries for help. It's none of your business. Don't get involved. You could get hurt. In the worst, most crime-ridden cesspools of cities, they used to coach women to scream "FIRE!" if they were being assaulted instead of calling for help. Fire, it turned out, was safer to watch than a violent rape in progress. Fire would not shoot or stab you just for seeing it and was therefore worth going out of one's way to see.

We pay very close attention to any call of alarm now, do we not? Not that we're any more inclined to help. Quite the contrary. When you hear cries for help, there are essential questions that need to be answered, and as quickly as possible.

How far away is the trouble, and in what direction?

What kind of creature might it be?

Can we grab our gear and slink away quietly, or must we drop everything and run?

Which way should we go?

That last one is critical. Wouldn't want to misjudge and run into danger instead of away and add your voice to the choir of agony.

It's been three years since the first monsters turned up, and it's safe to say they are here to stay. At least there's been no indication thus far that salvation lies ahead, whether it be some new, all-powerful weapon or divine intervention. As if there's ever been a difference. If there is a God, and He is watching, He is laughing long and hard... as He always has.

Were you close to one of the hot spots when things went to hell? As if things hadn't already gone to shit, what with most of the human race having been exterminated virtually overnight. Most people still can't believe that Tether was behind all that. In contrast, I cannot imagine who else could have pulled it off. Eighty percent of the world's population dropped to the ground like puppets with their strings cut, while another couple million were simultaneously eaten alive from the inside out. What other entity could have been so thorough? The monsters in our streets might as well have the Tether logo tattooed on their hides.

Was seeing a monster, as they were early on, a disappointment for you? Did you know in that moment that you were witnessing what amounted to the last stage of the End Of All Things? Of this, I also had no doubt. Somehow I sensed that we were well and truly fucked. If anything, I'm surprised that it took as long as it did to happen. Civilization had been on a steady downward spiral for almost a century.

Like so many animals before us, we've finally made the endangered species list. In fact, we're at the very top. The monsters do their best to keep us there, and they do it well.

What an enigma. They are dangerous, of course, but nobody can deny how interesting they are. If the intent was to throw one last fastball pitch to close out the apocalypse, Tether couldn't have done better.

But even knowing who was responsible for the ending of billions of human lives and the Ultimatum, there is still no clear reason as to why. Talking heads worldwide enthusiastically spouted their theories on any network that would have them, hoping to be correct.

Among the first and most popular of the multitude of conspiracy theories was that the monsters were bio-weapons, let loose to mop up anybody who was left from the first two attacks. Biologists who ascribed to this were labeled just as crazy as those who blamed aliens, the wrath of god, global warming, white privilege, or any of a host of other wacky notions.

In hindsight, the weapons theory makes the most sense to me. It is a scientific, pragmatic solution, and solving problems is what humans have always done best. Tether, in particular, did it better than anybody in the world. Sadly, the debaters will never know, as most are surely as dead as everybody else. It must be said that the one thing that all legitimate scientists shared in common, regardless of any variation in their beliefs, was that each of them did their best to warn people to do whatever they needed to do to protect themselves.

Though the theories are irrelevant now, one crucial aspect remains true. Monsters prefer us. I have seen ogres bypass herds of fat, juicy livestock just to catch and eat one skinny, miserable human. It is aberrant behavior. In the animal kingdom, it is a tactic used only by sick, injured, or old carnivores who can no longer do otherwise. There is little doubt that monsters were designed with humans in mind.

I find it fascinating.

Somebody, or a group of somebodies, put a great deal of thought into making creatures that would meticulously wipe out as much of an enemy country's population as possible while leaving most other life forms mostly intact. It's how I would have done it, except for the egregious oversight that the science project somehow jumped the fence and is now quite literally doing its best to eat every remaining human being on the planet.

I'm not complaining, by the way, if it seems like it. I'm good with things as they are. It's not as if our gene pool didn't need some chlorine, and monsters have undoubtedly made us a better, more robust species. But for the inconvenience of now having to constantly outthink things that want to eat me, the collapse of the old world was no great loss. When things went sideways, I was already alone in all the ways that mattered.

I wasn't abused, mind you, before you waste any time pitying me. Nothing could be further from the truth. In fact, my situation was quite the opposite. It just so happens that my parents were obscenely wealthy. They were Arab-royalty rich, and by default, so was I.

The downside was that they were old enough to have been my grandparents. I gathered that my arrival came as an unexpected and not altogether welcome surprise. They'd loved one other first, best, and always, and had been quite happy with the life they'd worked so hard to forge.

Day to day, our family life was normal, or so I assume. I don't know that there has ever been a baseline for "normal" where families are concerned. We talked a lot, laughed at things, took pictures for holiday cards, and had amazing vacations. I wanted for nothing, but an intangible something always separated them from me; invisible but every bit as solid and insurmountable as the towering stone walls that surrounded our domestic grounds. I feel like I was always aware of that barrier but came to terms with it when I was still very young - a blessing and curse of intelligence, I suppose.

Ultimately, Paul and Stella Carroway were two pleasant executive professionals who lived with me on our estate. We spent time together whenever they weren't working or traveling. My mother had a beautiful singing voice, and my father had a propensity for inappropriate humor. I inherited the latter but not the former. They were serious people who'd had neither the time nor desire to babysit. Neither had ever raised their voice in anger, let alone disciplined me. Nor did they ever change a diaper. All such unpleasant or boring aspects of raising a child were handled by a small, formidable army of world-class nannies and other staff.

Looking back, I believe they loved me as much as they could, and that's about all a person can ask of another. I can't and won't create reasons to condemn them for slights, real or imagined. I've fared better in life than most, especially considering I was technically a second child.

My folks were bound body and soul to their firstborn, Tether Corporation. Yes, that Tether, the same one that once touched basically every single civilized person on earth with its philanthropy, only to go on and commit murder on a scale that surpassed genocide. There isn't even a word that accurately describes it. Annihilation is probably as close as it gets. For obvious reasons, my family's legacy is something that I do not share with anyone.

Mother and Father weren't simply a part of Tether. They were One and Two of Tether's Seven original founding members. I knew them all, of course, as they were regular fixtures in our home. Each had been introduced to me as a number instead of a name. "This is Mr. Three and Mrs. Four." I found it amusing, as any child would, but it was not a joking matter whatsoever. The Seven always referred to one another numerically, both in person and when absent, and so did I. Despite the charade, I knew who many of them were, of course. It is impossible for those of a certain level of wealth to avoid notoriety, so it was no surprise to see the Strahans, Kadverians, Tysons, and Carroways on television now and again.

Though I was never among the "numbered," I spent as much time in their presence as possible, eavesdropping on their cryptic conversations and learning their mannerisms. Given the company we kept, it's no surprise that I never found other children interesting. Not when I had so many alluring, charismatic strangers as my occasional companions.

I sometimes wonder if I may one day have found myself seated at the Council's profoundly influential table, perhaps inducted as a fraction or decimal. "Everyone, please welcome our newest member, Mr. One-Point-Five." I will likely never know. Until the Ultimatum was broadcast, I had assumed that they were all dead, along with my parents. They might yet live, but finding one another in this world would be quite the feat. For a brief time, they were the most sought-after people to ever exist; the focus of every remaining intelligence, law enforcement, and military asset on Earth.

The prevailing theory among the survivors is that the Council was never composed of humans but an A.I. entity, which ultimately decided that the Transition was the best overall solution. It's difficult for me to even begin to know what's real, considering that all of the Seven went missing long before the Transition and the monsters that followed. It happened during one of their frequent business trips - allegedly - and not so much as a single screw from the corporate jet that carried them was ever found.

I can't say that it wasn't a difficult time for me, and I still miss them, but it wasn't nearly as traumatic as it might have been. When they disappeared, I was a child, but only in years. In terms of maturity, I was an adult in my own right, undoubtedly due to their influence, but perhaps not accidentally. They must have recognized that I'd have to be more self-sufficient than the average kid because they wouldn't be around for me - if for no other reason than their advanced age.

Irrespective of the cause for their early departure from my life, they were more correct than they could've imagined, and I'd thank them if I could.

Their entire estate passed to me, and they could not have left me better endowed. Armored in wealth that exceeded that of many countries, I began blazing the trails of my life. Having become, virtually overnight, one of the wealthiest people on the planet, I was free to pursue a curious and diverse array of interests and recreational pursuits.

If anyone had known of even half of the things I got away with and the lengths I went to keep them hidden, it would have made me the envy of any covert operations unit on the planet. And quite possibly a target. I wasn't overly concerned, for the ultra-wealthy have always enjoyed a level of protection inconceivable to the common man.

Though privileged, I was fundamentally different from everybody I ever knew. I was always cognizant of that fact and comfortable with it, but never were my eccentricities more stark than during my years at the academy. My story, such as it was, preceded me. I was a celebrity before I even passed through the high, medieval doors of Abruzzi Academy. If you've never heard of the Abruzzi, I'm not surprised. As preparatory institutions went, it was *the* school, as storied in status as academia.

My name alone made me the epicenter of privileged society, but the fact that I owned my wealth outright fascinated my fellow students. The professors and other staff must have been pissing themselves, dreading the day I darkened their door like the coming of the antichrist himself. If I had chosen so, I could have been a legend by the time I graduated. I was never interested in status, however, and that was something a lot of my elitist classmates never could wrap their little heads around.

It confounded them that I did not blow small fortunes on parties, drugs, and material things. People I did not know would stop me in the halls and ask me, gravely seriously, why I even bothered with school at all. I could take ecstasy and have a threesome in the middle of a biology lecture, and the professor would sooner incorporate it into the lesson plan than dare to interrupt me. One kid told me in a whisper that I could probably murder a teacher in a classroom full of people and get away with it. That is particularly funny, looking back.

The issue was that preoccupation with status was a very serious thing at the time and an avaricious monster in its own right. People had somehow come to believe that status equated to intelligence and an indefinable superiority. Brand names were held in higher regard than doctorates.

TETHERED

Striding the halls of Abruzzi and listening to the conversations taking place beneath me was the intellectual equivalent of stepping barefoot into warm, squishy piles of shit. I felt that if I'd ever acknowledged it, I would never be able to get it out from between my toes.

The height of most communication was gossip, centered on actors, music "artists" and reality television personalities, some of whom had criminal records thicker than their collective academic awards would ever be. There was no shortage of bad behavior amongst the student body and, in some instances, outright felonious activity. None of it ever surprised me, but what really blew my mind sometimes was how many kids got caught doing the ridiculous things they did.

I've always held firm that anybody stupid enough to get caught doing anything they wished to keep hidden was unworthy of serious consideration. And nothing was weaker or more pathetic to me than a cry for attention from a trust fund baby.

It goes without saying that few people could understand the plane upon which I existed, let alone function there. Where we crossed paths academically, they could not compete at all. Even when dealing with professors and administrators, I was often compelled to take the higher road of simply keeping it to myself whenever I knew more about a subject than those teaching it. Which was often. Like all Carroways, I was a glutton for knowledge. One of my favorite teachers was a physics professor who referred to me as "a voracious, bell-curve wrecking terror."

Had I been born into another socioeconomic realm and attended any regular public school, I would have been considered a freak, but I don't think the extremely wealthy are ever called freaks, and certainly not to their faces. If there is an alternative name it remains unknown to me. I was, however, considered odd, and rightly so, for any one of multiple good reasons.

Rather than seek chemically induced fun amid the throngs of wealthy addicts, I was an outdoorsman, and I traveled quite a bit in pursuit of it. My "backyard" was basically a national park in its own right; a couple hundred acres of heavily forested land dotted with hills, mountains, lakes, and rivers that belonged to me alone. Aside from certain other benefits that I will not get into, I much preferred the solitude only the deep forest seems to provide. I came to value the challenge of discovering life's many unknowns rather than following paths worn by countless unknown feet. Years of biking, hiking, and climbing had made my body as hard as granite, and I had the stamina of an Iditarod dog.

All the way through to summa cum laude, I left sad, frustrated coaches in my wake, lamenting my disinclination towards organized sports. In stature, I was at eye level with most basketball players but heavier and more muscular than any football player or wrestler. I could run half the cross-country kids into the dust. I can not overstate the importance of being able to outrun other people in today's world.

I understand this is a bit of a ramble. Still, it's important to the narrative in that I was exempt from the outright harassment I might have endured, no matter the environment, due to my being a very large and physically imposing oddity. Consequently, I have no personal horror stories about bullying. Other than dirty looks and hushed mutterings in my direction, I was only tested once.

The kid's name was Hollister, and everyone called him Holli. He was roughly my height, but narrower in the shoulder. He was also soft as warm butter from too much mirror time and video gaming. I knew of him, but he was just one among hundreds of other students with whom I shared nothing in common. I have no idea what his specific issue was. Jealousy? Perhaps. Ultimately, he decided he didn't like me... which would have been fine if he'd kept it to himself. But people like Holli did not keep things to themselves.

The verbal harassment had begun some time before, unprovoked, and became a regular part of my daily life. I ignored his insults, as was my habit in dealing with all irrelevant people, and soon refused to even acknowledge his existence. Holli had probably never been ignored in his entire life, particularly not with such casual disregard. To me, he might as well have been a hair stuck to the back of a urinal, something to look upon with a hint of disgust and then forgotten. Inevitably, it became too much for him to process, and he decided he needed to teach me a physical lesson.

There's no telling what he expected to come of it, but he quickly learned that life is not like a video game. Within a half second of touching me, he found himself snatched off his feet, shaken like a sock monkey and then flung a distance that was surprising to him, me, and the approximately fifty or so other people who'd happened to stop and watch the show.

He slid down the freshly waxed hall floor, coasting in a highly undignified manner, past an assemblage of wide-eyed students and teachers. His momentum was finally stopped by a wall of lockers, and some legendary soul made an off-the-cuff remark that he looked like the Curling Stone of Regret. From that day forth, he became known as 'Curly' and would bear that nickname for the remaining two years.

By noon the next day, students had begun forming 'human curling' teams. They broke into maintenance closets for mops and brooms, and 'sweeping' Curly's path to class became so common that he spent weeks late to almost every class.

The administration tired of the affair quickly and forbade it, which only encouraged it to the point where 'teams' were showing up in uniforms they'd had made expressly for that purpose. At the height of its popularity, one of the team 'captains' petitioned for time to practice in the gym after school. Despite my lack of involvement, I lost count of how many times I was asked to coach.

Curly hadn't been well-liked, so there wasn't much in the way of grief when he died in a bizarre car accident halfway through our junior year. His was the first in a series of deaths that left the entire school shaken long after our class had moved on to bigger and better things.

Suffice it to say there weren't many people interested in putting their hands on me after the Curling incident, which worked out best for everyone. Others were not so fortunate as I, and it amazes me to this day just how unequipped most people were to defend themselves on any functional level.

You wouldn't think that bullying would have been as common among the wealthy, but if anything, it was worse. Physical beatings were rare but often violent and mostly swept under the rug or bought into nonexistence. Affluent mommies and daddies who contributed to their children's schools always knew how to make their money work for them. Let me just say that given some of the cruelty I'd witnessed, I'm surprised that school shootings weren't more common.

As an interesting aside to this story, it would come to my attention now and again that some "loser" had been spared a beating on the grounds that they were assumed to be my friend. I never made friends, per se, but I was part of a vague general grouping of students understood to be Them, which is significant only in that it differs from Us. That association was somehow interpreted as camaraderie.

I never denied it, of course. I'm not an asshole, just a realist. There were a handful of people with whom I'd quietly shared common interests. Of those, I knew only one well enough to consider anything close to a friend.

The guy's name was Ben Rutton. I suspect that he may have been as intelligent as I was. He was smart enough to get a full ride through MIT, anyway, which is the only way he would have ever seen it. He'd come from a blue-collar family - people who many elites considered, financially speaking, an "untouchable" caste.

He was no such person, of course, but it made him a target, and he caught more hell from the elitists than anyone I'd ever seen. He'd been number one on Curly's list until he decided he'd had enough. Never have I seen anyone verbally sodomize another so consistently or thoroughly or with such enthusiasm.

Ben revealed himself to be the William Shakespeare of tongue-lashing. He made a spectacular punching bag of Curly daily, much to the delight of the entire school. It got fairly awful for Ben towards the end, to the point where I had finally decided to intercede on his behalf. It would prove unnecessary, for it was around that time that Curly and most of his inner circle began dying their strange, messy deaths.

If anyone had ever benefitted from the gruesome death of others, it was Ben. Whenever I think of him, I often wonder if he'd had anything to do with the whole grisly business. He was never officially implicated in any of the accidents – if that's what they were – which, by the way, were some of the most violent, uniformly grisly, and spectacularly horrendous incidents I'd ever heard of. For all that I knew him, Ben was gentle and well-spoken, and it seemed improbable that a person like that could orchestrate such mayhem...short of using voodoo. I know better now the depths to which people will go to preserve their wellbeing. We all do.

Whether he did or didn't, everyone regarded Ben differently afterward. There was an unspoken understanding that he made the list of Those Not To Be Fucked With, where he remained through to graduation and beyond. I'd be willing to bet that he's still alive somewhere and, like me, getting along just fine.

Many "losers" seem to fare rather well in this new world. One rarely becomes a winner without obstacles. It has always been the case; a fact that soft, privileged people seldom learn. Now, possibly more than ever, we must earn our place.

And speaking of winners, here you are, presumably alone, unless of course some of the kids were still here when you arrived. I find that unlikely, but there will undoubtedly be obvious evidence of their habitation. You're curious either way, I'm sure, but don't worry, I'm getting to it.

I've decided to write this brief memoir because I find myself with both time and means and the unusual luxury of being bored. I might have used colored construction paper and crayons to illustrate, but no crayons were left, and it didn't seem right to use one without the other. The crayons were long gone before I got here and put to good use, judging by the scattering of poorly colored pictures likely still lying about.

It's also possible that the crayons were eaten. Not because there was a lack of food, mind you. There's almost certainly still food here, but I know that once upon a time, there had been kids who would eat crayons.

My parents may have had some justifiable concerns about my behavior during childhood, but rest assured they never worried about me eating crayons, glue, or paint chips. I never ingested things that were obviously not intended for consumption. I don't recall using crayons even to color. I always preferred colored pencils or watercolor, but to each their own.

You can be sure that the crayon-eaters of the world are long gone. They went hand in hand with the mirror-gazers, video gamers, and safe-space seekers. Admittedly, the conditions that transpired to dispose of them were extreme, but we are well rid of them nonetheless.

The tragedy in all of it, if any, is that despite a growing number of those sorts, we as a species had been heading to a place of unprecedented enlightenment and development. We were 3D printing new bodies and had been on the verge of downloading our very consciousness. It almost seemed that the universe at large observed some sudden spike in human idiocy and decided to take a hand in restoring equilibrium... but had gotten a bit carried away.

We were standing upon the very threshold of immortality, and now we may as well be back to using sticks and stones, as Einstein once predicted. There is undeniable irony in that only the most intelligent of us could have been capable of catapulting us so far backward. As a point of fact, some of us do use sticks and stones as weapons, and anything else we can get our hands on when things go badly.

You do what you have to do to survive; otherwise, something will eventually run you down, and you will be noisily and messily consumed. Regardless of all you've ever hoped to have become in life, your efforts will literally amount to shit; a big, steaming pile of reeking monster shit with pieces of clothing sticking out.

And how about these monsters? Even I, blessed with such vivid imagination and prodigious intellect, could not have designed better. Seeing that first of the many bizarre monstrosities to come was possibly the most profound and significant event of my entire life.

I'd felt its presence long before I ever spotted it. Not everyone to fun afoul of larvae knows the sensation. If you haven't experienced it yourself, it's difficult to put into words. For me, at least, it came as an intense flash of overwhelming, all-encompassing discomfort. I would describe it as psychological nausea. The ability to generate it was strongest in the larvae, but all monsters can still do it to lesser or greater degrees. It is much the same way that weasels and snakes mesmerize their prey, but far more powerfully focused.

Likewise, some people are more sensitive to it than others. I still get a tingle every time one gets close, thank the gods. I wouldn't give up my premonitory bubble guts for anything. The occasional feeling that my brain is going to shit itself is always going to be preferable to being torn apart.

It's safe to say there are few, if any, people left who do not possess this ability in some form or another. When interviewed in ambulances (or hospitals if they were lucky enough to make it that far), the few who'd managed to survive a physical attack had one thing in common: they did not recall experiencing that foreboding feeling of mental sickness that so many others did.

TETHERED

My first encounter happened while I was biking. I didn't even see it at first and might have passed it by completely had I not sensed it. It was just off a popular trail where the brush started to thicken, a formless lump roughly the size and shape of a basketball. My first thought upon spotting it was that it was garbage. I could never in good conscience ignore litter, and moron tourists, or tourons as we thought of them, were always throwing trash on the ground, treating the whole world like a dump. Think what you will about Tether, but there's no denying they found a way to deal with problems like that.

It was immediately apparent that not only was the thing definitely not garbage - it was unlike anything I'd ever seen. My first thought was that it was an unusually beat-up roadkill or some half-eaten something left by a coyote or mountain lion, but neither felt right. It looked like something had been burned alive and then turned inside out, then left to suffer as a pile of glistening meat and organs, quivering in agony. Regardless of how it had come to be in that condition, I decided the right thing to do was to put it out of its misery.

I pictured myself doing just that - finding a big rock or stick to bash it; or perhaps stomp it until it was dead. Find something. Come closer. Yes, that's what I had to do; I was sure of it. Closer. It was as though I could hear it: a wordless, urgent command. But some voice of warning came fully awake then, screaming soundlessly and freezing me in my tracks. I remember deciding that whatever it was, the unfortunate critter would just have to tough it out until it died. I had just begun to back my bike onto the trail when I was overcome by an intense euphoria.

Movement caught my eye, and I was surprised to see that the thing was no longer simply gyrating but was now moving along the ground towards me. The words 'meat jello' popped into my mind, and it was absurd enough to make me chuckle out loud. I remember hearing the sound of my own laughter as if from a great distance, distorted and echoing, and I lost track of what I was about.

When I returned to my senses, I was alarmed to find myself much closer - and the thing still creeping in my direction. Worse, I had begun to move as well, slowly but surely closing the distance between. The meat jello was quivering in anticipation, pulsing softly and comfortingly in the dusk like a lightning bug. Bursts of soft, reddish light emanated from somewhere deep in its center and came in time with my own heartbeat, like a lava lamp. *Larva Lamp*, I'd thought to myself and giggled again. I had to physically shake myself to get a grip. It was the mental equivalent of trying to pry myself out of a huge, sticky rodent trap. Once my head cleared, the sense of being lulled leveled off. There was just a hint of it left, like the smell of a distant campfire. The experience reminded me of something.

My family and I had often spent time on the beaches and bays all along the Atlantic coast, where crabbing was a considerable part of the local culture. If you don't know, it's like fishing. You tie a string to a chicken leg or some other bait (preferably smelly), drop it in the water and let it sink to the bottom. When a crab starts tugging at it, you draw it up slowly, waiting with a wire net to snag it once it comes into sight. Not being completely stupid, the crabs would drop off your bait if you moved too fast. That's how it felt, except I was the crab, and whatever that thing was pulling me had jumped the gun. I couldn't have known at the time, but the incident was merely the first of many close encounters to come.

What I recall most, and which remains of greatest significance, is that the air seemed to crackle with a faint static, like walking too close to high-voltage power lines. It is a sensation that I still get every time monsters are near. I've met others who experience it, but none as intensely as I do. I didn't think much on it for a long time, much less consider what it might represent. Now I know.

I think I will pick this back up in the morning. I'd have to make light to keep writing. Even if your formal education does not cover optics, you may still know that all artificial light is unnatural and that we are the only things that make it. The kids I found know it, and they've kept things in here as dark as possible because the monsters sure as hell know it, too.

Good morning.

Did you sleep? I do not, even though it's supposed to be impossible for humans. Medical science established long ago that sleep served a greater purpose than just allowing a body to rest and recharge. If a person doesn't sleep, they cannot dream. When a human being doesn't dream, they will eventually die. Normal, healthy brains need their downtime, or else. Unsurprisingly, sleep deprivation was once among the most effective forms of interrogation and was used by intelligence organizations all over the world.

If you keep the average person awake and completely alert for three days, they will tell you anything you want to know. I once found that difficult to believe until I spent most of the first several months of my life in the new world almost constantly awake. I get it now. I'm a fast learner, too. Indeed, I have adapted far more rapidly than anyone should.

I don't think I have dreams anymore; if I do, I no longer remember them. And I still don't sleep. It's more like a state of deep meditation. I think there is a part of my mind that's always been particularly attuned to my environment, although I now seem to be even more aware of the world around me. I noticed it was becoming increasingly more substantial, like a muscle that gets daily exercise, but it's evolved well beyond that. Now it feels almost like a separate identity that watches out for me.

Perhaps my brain just understands that it's necessary, which it absolutely is, but however it came about, it has saved my ass on more occasions than I can remember...especially at night. Humans are at our weakest at night, the most vulnerable, and in all the wild history of predators, those that prowl in darkness have always been the most feared. As far as saving ass goes in general, any attribute that bolsters caution is most welcome. From my point of view, there has always been a profound deficit of caution in most people.

College biology may no longer be relevant or particularly useful anymore, but common sense is more important than ever. Having a strong sense of self-preservation is a must. Most people have always instinctively known better than to get cuddly with any unknown organism, and that especially applies to things that are brightly colored or possessed of fangs, spines, or stingers. Unfortunately, never has everyone been rational. There have always been slow learners and the special few here and there who refuse to learn at all.

Death By Unwise Pet Selection is not an issue anymore, what with so many dangerous things around, but there were always those in the world gone by who could not resist the pull of strange and dangerous things. There were countless stories of people killed by things that were never intended to be pets. Folks were routinely bitten and poisoned by insects, reptiles, and other things they chose to keep in their own homes. In rare instances, an individual would be devoured by a pet bear or lion, much to the glee of many social media enthusiasts.

Oddly, the more exotic the creature happened to be, the stronger the attraction often was. No matter how grotesque something might appear, somebody would inevitably want to touch it. It was among the first things the faster-developing monsters learned. And they are still learning.

Monsters 101 has a steep learning curve, to say the least. People must learn quickly, or else. The predators who now rule the world are their own special category of dangerous. They are better hunters and trackers than any creature I've ever studied. They can be deceptively creative, and do not conform to the familiar, accepted laws of nature. They never did, and the last mistake you'll ever make is assuming they are like other animals.

Before I get too involved in the specifics of describing monsters, I'd like to get back to my brief encounter, as it's important to the end. It ended with me snapping a few pics with my phone, climbing back on my bike, and leaving, with constant looks over my shoulder. Under normal circumstances, my sighting would have been relegated to the same drawer containing brittle polaroids of frisbee UFOs and grainy Bigfoot and Nessie videos (which were somehow always shot with the shittiest cameras available at the time).

But circumstances were as far from normal as they could be and unlikely to ever return to how they were. There was no government in America or elsewhere. However, there were still a few individuals out there with enough authority that people with guns were following their orders. Within days, I was attached to a team for an expedition to my 'ground zero.' Square miles had been evacuated of the few survivors who remained, and the area was dotted with militia outposts. Most of these were rudimentary, but those closest to the trail were balls out, with fortified trenches and bunkers supported by heavy weapons.

Despite the chaos into which we'd suddenly been plunged, the Lab Coats were excited, and I suppose I was too, for a time. But my enthusiasm waned considerably when I realized the soldiers and law enforcement were scared. Actually, in the interest of accuracy, they were terrified. Terror is easy to recognize. One hopes to never see it, especially when it's barely controlled and straining the fortitude of battle-hardened combat veterans. It was as sobering as falling through thin ice, watching their hands white-knuckled and trembling on their weapons. They were locked and loaded like they'd been told to expect dinosaurs. Whoever gave them their operation brief hadn't been far off the mark. That's when I understood that things hadn't gotten as bad as they could be.

I had a college acquaintance who was Army ROTC, finishing his degree for Warrant Officer school. He wasn't the sharpest guy I knew, but he happened to share my fondness for philosophy. He always seemed more concerned with theorizing why a problem existed than finding solutions. I doubt that he's still among us. Anyway, he was proud of his extensive military training and would speak of it in depth after a few beers. He frequently expressed that certain schools and training had taught him more about himself than the skills that were actually intended. I couldn't agree more. Even the most realistic training is still simulation, and will always have limitations in real-world applications. You know nothing until you're tested for real.

The entire world has become a crucible – its people forged anew and of far stronger mettle. Even the purest pacifists in history must have secretly wondered their limits. Survivors do what's necessary to survive, and we do it well. Unthinkable actions are now standard procedure. My advice is to not dwell on it. Speculation is even more worthless than theoretical education.

Speaking of speculation, I don't have a clue as to where the monsters actually came from or why they're here. Somebody might be trying to figure it out, but I'm not Darwin, and these aren't finches. I have pursued some pretty unorthodox courses of study, but the only research that matters to me anymore is that which helps me survive. It's been liberating in a way, and I've been pleasantly surprised to have found all of my 'real-world' education to be intellectually and physically more challenging than any other I've experienced.

It was always taken for granted that we would eventually experience another global catastrophe, but nobody outside science fiction writers could have foreseen the scope and magnitude of the terrors to come. H.G. Wells would shit his pants if he could see this. None of us were ready, but to be fair, some things defy preparation.

"Here There Be Monsters." Isn't that what the old sailors' maps used to have scrawled in the uncharted areas? That's where we are now. Off the map. And there are no stars to guide us back.

In case you don't, there are specifics about monsters that you should know. First, they are very much the antithesis of the natural order. Strengths evolve over time to give an animal an edge in some ways while leaving it vulnerable in others. We expected monsters to comply with these rules, and in some ways they did, but not nearly long enough. Also, and most unfortunately, they don't have much in the way of a corresponding lack of strengths.

Monsters have somehow borrowed the most useful traits from the other families of the former animal kingdom, like venom, spines, and armor, without absorbing any specific vulnerability. They are exceedingly difficult to destroy. Once, if you had problems with coyotes, mountain lions, hogs, or bears, you could shoot them. If your guns weren't up to the task of getting rid of a specific animal, you could buy bigger ones or better ammunition until something did the trick. It's not so simple as that anymore.

All monsters are apex predators regardless of size or shape, and they have been specifically, and in some cases, spitefully designed to last. The word impervious comes to mind. Old-world bullets do not stop or even marginally discourage the dominant breeds. Anything with a gelatinous body will shrug off small-arms projectiles like gnats, or simply absorb and digest them. If you shoot at something unusually massive and solid, you're far more likely to piss that something off and have it after you than you are to kill it. So don't do that.

All monsters are always hungry, or so it seems, constantly sniffing, peering about, and tasting the air. I've mentioned their preference for human meat. Even heavy snoring gets people eaten. Thankfully, my roommates know to stay nice and quiet. Kids have better instincts than we give them credit for, mostly - but no child's imagination could have held a candle to the reality in which we live.

The monster kingdom is diverse, and their individual biologies are fascinating. One kind casts out fine, ultra-light filaments like a spider's web that can spin out for miles. We call them Flyfishers. Wind won't trigger their webs, nor disturbances from any non-animal, but if anything larger than a squirrel so much as brushes against a strand, it will become stuck. I've seen plenty of 'Fishers up close and more personally than I'd like. When they show up to check their lines, the prey spends its last moments wishing it was something only as awful as a gigantic spider. No matter what the species, we are constantly faced with the issue of how to fight them.

In our rise to the top, humans grew physically weaker but had come to depend on our intellect to give us the edge. We developed weapons – universal solutions to exploit the weaknesses common to all animals. We started with stones, clubs, and spears, eventually moving to fire and projectile weapons. Science was experimenting with focused energy weapons when the Transition came and wiped the slate clean. Now, we are often hard-pressed to find guns and ammo, let alone anything advanced. Thankfully, we still have electricity. In sufficient amounts, it is enough to kill just about anything, but it is not always dependable. Most power grids have been inoperable for years, and some monsters instinctively destroy any that are restored.

Thankfully, fire remains a friend to us and at least somewhat effective against almost everything. It is lethal to some creatures, and Dreds are the perfect example of why you should never be without the means of making it.

Dreds are one of the species I consider Permanent Residents. They are among the most common things out there and definitely the most distinguishable. They were, as far as we can determine, the first species to have settled quickly on a successful form, and they've established themselves as a heavy-hitter in the food chain. Almost every other type of monster will go out of its way to avoid one, and that says the most about how dangerous they are.

There's one outside this compound right now, in fact, sloshing around in the mud since the day after I arrived. I've come to think of it as Bob. (You may or may not get the reference.)

Dreds are indestructible except for their susceptibility to fire. A building could fall on Bob, and it would wiggle out and go about its business as though nothing had happened. I've seen combat helicopters shoot tank-killer rounds into them with zero effect. They ignore physical trauma of any sort, but if I were to throw a torch at this one right now, it would go up like a Roman Candle and be immolated in minutes.

When it all started, the majority of people who died were killed while trying to pet or play with little Dreds. There were videos all over YouTube before the internet went down with the rest of the infrastructure. The most famous footage was a live broadcast, accidentally aired, that showed a drunken cowboy in South Dakota trying to ride one on a bet. Even with armageddon well in progress, folks still found time to comment on social media in typical epic fashion. *See? Some cowboys will ride anything if they're drunk enough. Y'all hairy-ass bitches still have a chance!*

One would think that people would have been even more on guard, but nothing could be further from the truth. There was panic, but not nearly to the degree it was warranted. There weren't really any casualties from the Transition attacks, but all of the functioning emergency centers soon found themselves full to capacity, where doctors tried unsuccessfully to remove puppy-sized Dreds from their victims.

None of this was surprising to most survivors I've spoken with. We as a society had seen so much violence and death in the preceding decades that many people had become inured to even the worst atrocities. There were countless hours of online footage of human-on-human crime. Much of that featured other people standing around, sometimes only feet away, watching...and sometimes recording with their camera phones.

With technology so advanced, it had become often impossible to tell the real thing from Hollywood. People commented on social media platforms that seeing people get destroyed by monsters in real life was "actually kind of boring" compared to their favorite horror movies.

After watching generations of adorable creatures on the big and small screens, I can see how it could be difficult for some people to be alarmed by something that looks like the cute offspring of a sloth and a slinky. The problem is that, when it comes to Dreds, it's what's inside that counts. Underneath its mad tangle of hairy tentacles is something that latches on. It might be a claw, or suckers like you'd find on a squid, or something that I can't even imagine.

They also have no difficulty snaring multiple victims at once, much to the unfortunate dismay and horror of all first responders who tried to help. There have been people who, once caught in the carnivorous mop, have begged to be shot and put out of their misery. I strive to never find myself needing to make a decision like that.

Not even trauma doctors ever figured out what they are. Dreds cannot be removed from their victims and will not let go until they are finished feeding. It was considered unsafe to allow them to live. Since the remaining doctors had no time for research, all specimens were cremated with the human remains upon which they fed. It was the only way to ensure they would pose no further threat.

The only thing that keeps Dreds from being the most terrifying thing I've ever encountered is that they do not aggressively hunt. They seem to blunder into most meals, and will try to eat statues, bushes, old tires, or anything else they happen upon. They sample widely and ignore anything that doesn't seem edible. It's occurred to me that they might simply be dumb, but I'm not one for making assumptions. Plenty of monsters are as adept at feigning disinterest as others are at tracking and chasing. They could simply be patient and thorough. I'm all set with erring on the side of caution.

That is the extent of what I know about them, and they are the only species I know that much about, and that's only because Dreds are easy to safely observe. Seeing it written makes it seem suspiciously like I don't know much at all, but what is to be taken away from this is that they are the offspring of nightmares and must be avoided at all costs.

I want to reiterate that you should utilize avoidance as the primary tactic for anything dangerous, but this is especially true where Dragons are concerned.

They are the rarest of all monster species. If you should ever encounter one the best thing to do is freeze in place and, if you think it will help, pray that you haven't been spotted. The moment you're sure you have, you'd better run as though your life depends on it. There are Vegas odds that you will not survive a dragon attack, but that never means you shouldn't try.

So far as I know, I am the only person who ever has, except for the occasional liar who will claim to not only have survived an attack but to have actually killed them. This is not merely a bigger lie but a statement that crosses the line into the valley of preposterous bullshit. Interestingly, Dragons are unique among all other monsters in that they are the only ones to kill for sport. They have a great deal to do with the writing of this short memoir, so keep that in mind.

Meanwhile, try to apply what I've imparted thus far regarding my understanding of Dreds to potentially dozens of alien creatures. I have formed what I feel is a reasonable, albeit non-verifiable hypothesis.

One of the tenets of basic biology is that significant adaptation can take millions of years to happen. Some monsters manifested noticeable change in months - or even weeks. The very first larvae to be sighted weren't much more than featureless lumps, like my meat jello basketball, which indicates to me that they likely began as templates - biologically engineered sponges that were placed in strategic locations to determine how well and quickly they could insinuate themselves into new environments.

In that first year, we saw hundreds of new species, but after that, the variegation began to taper off. The dominant Residents, especially the Dragons, began to systematically weed out the less successful.

It would be interesting to see how biologists might have tracked monster evolution. They would first have needed to overcome the horror of being hunted, which is not likely, not to mention that even the most in-depth study would probably be useless.

Fortunately for those of us who remain, there are commonalities - else none of us would be here.

All monsters are carnivorous. Don't ever expect to see anything grazing. Also, all of the permanent Residents seem to be intensely territorial. Whether a species is social enough to hunt in packs or prefers solitude, they do not appear to mingle. Even if they tolerate the presence of their own kind, all monsters flee or fight when they encounter any other species. If there's a fight, the loser is always eaten. I have observed no cannibalization following same-species combat, which I cannot puzzle out.

Apart from the Residents, there is, or was, a vague subgroup of creatures I think of as Things - creatures that couldn't decide what they wanted to be. There aren't many of these around now - their numbers having been efficiently pruned by the more effective Residents. This is not important. If you survive long enough, you may begin to recognize differences between the Residents and Things, but what is of major importance is that all of the Things left are bat-shit crazy... and the most attracted by noise. Never has the term "silence is golden" been more meaningful.

It should go without saying that you should be as quiet as possible as often as possible. But, should anything get after you, or you find yourself trapped - make as much racket as humanly possible. It might seem contrary, but you have to attract attention. Things will *always* hear and investigate a potential free meal.

Even if they are hopelessly outmatched, Things will immediately attack any other monster they encounter, and once they start they do not stop. It will kill or be killed, eat or be eaten. In either case, both monsters ought to be busy enough for you to get away. You'd do well to get your ass out of there as soon as convenient in case the loser turns out to be an hors d'oeuvre.

It seems like a seat-of-the-pants strategy because it is, but our best decisions have almost always motivated by instinct. I've seen monsters kill everything that walks, swims, or flies, but they *want* to eat humans. I mentioned it before, but it's priority information and bears repeating. I'd burn that into your memory if I were you.

In general, rest when you can, gather supplies wherever you find them, never stay too long in one spot, and always be ready to bug out. Another thing that bears repeating is that sheltering or hiding will always be preferable to fighting.

It should go without saying that, though it is certainly a better option than being eaten, trapping yourself anywhere should be a last resort. Tough, reinforced structures are the best shelters, if you can find them. A bank vault or anything like it is ideal, except that there's generally only one way in or out.

This military bunker I found is a best case scenario all around, but good luck finding any that aren't already occupied. You may presume that any people already occupying these sorts of places are more intelligent, ruthless, and dangerous than any monster.

In my opinion, the skill of being able to hide is the most valuable of all. If something cannot find you, it cannot harm you. I've proven to be a natural when it comes to this, perhaps from my years of being unobtrusive. I can vanish like a chameleon's ghost when I need to, which is often.

I might be beating a dead horse, but I could never overstate the intelligence of monsters, or how infinitely patient they can be. Some of will wait hours, days, or even weeks for someone to come out of a hidey-hole. The bright side is that even the most patient of them might eventually lose interest - or find something else to eat.

The most enormous and powerful monsters are the Giants... and they don't wait for anything. I'm not sure how to estimate their raw strength mostly because nothing comes remotely close - I've seen them tear apart shipping containers like wet cardboard. You could only wish that something so big would be slow.

Ogres are the largest, and will pummel any shelter until they gets in. If the process of gaining entry does not turn you into a bloody bag of dead meat, you can look forward to being eaten feet first. After you stop squawking, and only then, the Ogre will pop off your head - like a child with a dandelion - and crunch it up like a jawbreaker.

Where Ogres prefer eating their victims alive and kicking, Trolls favor slow constriction. They squeeze victims, slurping the innards out of whichever major orifice gives way first. I've seen it, and nothing reinforces the importance of having a solid backup plan like watching that go down. The sound alone is unforgettable.

About a year into this nightmare, I saw an ex-Marine shoot a Troll - and contrary to my advice, I might add. In his defense, he had the use of a trackless tank, and declared with the utmost confidence that it would do the job just fine. I still get a chuckle out of the memory.

The guy, who insisted on being called Gunny even though he'd only been a Lance Corporal, popped up out of the turret of the immobilized vehicle and fired. The twenty-five foot tall, heavily armored Troll - which would have soon moved on without ever knowing we were there, took the shot beneath its shoulder plates. The explosion blew it through the wall of the building where it was poking about, leaving behind an arm and a huge puddle of piss, both of which were still on fire. The Marine had a good laugh over it... for the five seconds it took for the Troll's head to reappear.

I have no doubt that Gunny created his own considerable puddle while ducking back through the hatch. Too late. The Troll caught sight of him through the smoking void of choking dust and flame. With its three remaining arms it tore the turret off the tank as easily as popping the cap off a bottle of beer. Its hands were too big to get inside, so instead, it lifted the entire body of the tank and shook it until the squealing idiot fell out.

MICHAEL MUSTACHIO

All things considered, he was lucky. The Troll was in a rage and killed him almost immediately. We could hear things popping inside him from the high rooftop where the rest of us hid. Then, it stretched and beat him against the asphalt until he looked like a red sock. Human skin is much more resilient than one would think. Once sufficiently pulpy, the thing held him up by the feet and started squeezing him, working him down like it was trying to get the last bit of toothpaste out of a tube.

I've learned at least half of my survival skills from the bad examples of others, much like the one I just described. I carefully watch everything around me and choose my battles wisely. For example, I have no plans to set fire to Bob, who is currently visible outside the window directly in front of me. It has not bothered us, and I will extend the same courtesy. Under other circumstances, I might have already torched it, but the presence of that Rastafarian slinky is keeping other monsters, including smaller types of Dragons, well away from me. The enemy of my enemy is my friend, and I'll take that when I can get it.

I had no real agenda when I began this, but I want to expound on something else before I close. I could never have discussed this specific matter with anyone before, nor written it down out of concern that it would be found and read.

I've learned more about myself in this new world than any number of therapists, military training courses, meditation, or self-help programs could have imparted. I am a Survivor. If you really want to know what it takes and the extent to which a person must be willing to go, consider the following.

This building is impenetrable. It is daunting even for a structure on a military base. I'm no engineer or architect, but this is not some "just-in-case" facility. There can be no doubt that whoever built this fortress did so with armageddon in mind.

The exterior walls are poured concrete, ten feet thick, with a core of steel plates. The doors are solid titanium. All points of egress are so easily secured that even the youngest of the children can bar them manually.

When I checked for sight lines, I initially assessed that the windows were some sort of poured polymer. Then I noticed one of the kids sticking magnets to it. They're not glass at all. They're transparent steel. Imagine the military keeping a secret like that.

And speaking of secrecy, the weapons I found here are unlike anything I've ever seen, straight out of a sci-fi movie. I can't even figure out how to operate most of them, and I'm not going to risk trying. It would be a shame to accidentally explode myself in some tragic misfire just for the sake of curiosity (I'll leave that to you if you're feeling lucky.) The systems I can use are nothing short of magical, and I'm confident that they'll prove to be more than adequate to protect me during my trip.

There is food here to last years, perhaps even decades if managed carefully, and there are undoubtedly other resources to be discovered. Unfortunately, I have neither the time nor inclination to explore more. Furthermore, some parts of the facility are too well protected to get into without a protracted, noisy effort, and I have good reason to be especially quiet.

It's no wonder that somebody would choose this place to bring children. They are the future.

Guarding them and ensuring their wellbeing in this world gone to hell would be as honorable a way for a man to spend his days as any that might come to mind. Even without them to give existence a purpose, I could have stayed here indefinitely and found ways to make it truly impervious. I considered all these things, believe me.

Taking all into account, you must want to know why I'm not here to greet you in person. It's simple. There are a pair of Dragons tracking me, and not even Bob's presence outside will be enough to deter them.

TETHERED

I spoke of these creatures before. I'll elaborate now.

Dragons are the exception to the already exceptional. Their senses are otherworldly, and there is basically nothing you can do if one catches a whiff of you and decides it's going to have you. They have an uncanny tendency to get into places where they shouldn't be physically able without literally decreasing their mass, which they absolutely can do. If they can't get in, they will wait, and in human terms that basically means forever. Like Yours Truly, Dragons don't seem to need sleep, and people have starved in place waiting for a Dragon to go away.

They are more diverse than all the other types of animals combined. They can be smooth and slimy, armored, or have hide as coarse as sandpaper that will skin you to the bone. They may fly, swim, climb, tunnel, or run. Some do all of the above. Those that run (on two legs or as many as ten) can run down a high performance motorcycle.

Dragons are hands-down the smartest things that have ever walked this planet, and I doubt that anything even comes close. I'm sure they get bored of hunting and killing in the bountiful, target-rich environment they must regard this world to be.

In terms of durability, they are in a class by themselves. Let's say for the sake of argument that you stumble upon one and shoot it out of reflex before you can think better of it. Most likely, you will miss altogether because you're shitting in your pants...because you're looking at a Dragon. Shooting virtually guarantees that it will pinpoint your exact whereabouts, and at that point you should expend all ammunition. It's unlikely that you will be able to do more than slow it down, but at least you'll die trying.

Suppose you have an incendiary weapon and, by some chance, decide to hose a Dragon with fire. In that case, you will receive your last practical lesson on new-age biodiversity. Like their mythical namesakes of old, Dragons are very comfortable with fire. Most produce their own in one form or another, some hot enough to melt industrial diamonds. If attacked with fire, most will hunker down and wait for you to run out of whatever fuels the flame, or simply dodge the stream. There is one species that will open its mouth wide, suck in the flame, then spit it back at you mixed with bile, like a napalm Slurpee.

Because of Dragons, I have developed a severe aversion to anything even remotely reptilian in appearance. The arrival of any such creature is a worst-case scenario, and there is nothing I won't do to avoid or evade one.

Oh, another thing I should mention is that Dragons talk. Maybe it's something you've heard with your own ears. In case you haven't, let me clarify: I don't mean that they mimic humans or communicate in some sort of growling Dragon-speak that only they understand. They do appear to communicate that way, of course, but what I'm saying is that some Dragons can speak in human tongues... in multiple languages. I've watched them coax people out of hiding, crying and calling like a lost human child. "Heeeeeeeeelp meeeee. Pleeeaaaase heeeeeeelp."

I've learned much from observing Dragons and find them worthy of both awe and respect. They're almost invincible... almost. I discovered quite accidentally that they are, apparently, especially susceptible to even small amounts of electricity.

TETHERED

No living thing in this world has ever been able to survive electrocution, not even those rare species that could generate it. Not so the Monsters, who inexplicably tend to shrug it off. There are beasts among us now that could floss with live electric distribution cable. I assumed it to be a characteristic common to all Monsters until I saw a Dragon run afoul of a downed line. It was transfixed immediately, smoking as it cooked, and finally exploded in a shower of spines and gore.

Dragons often perch high up, like hawks - the better to locate prey. For some reason it never occurred to me that I'd never seen one climb a power pole or tower.

I set about the designing and fabrication of a taser, and never has my education proved more useful. It is powerful enough to drop a rhino, and instantly lethal to humans (you could draw your own conclusions here and probably be right.) The final test of the weapon, however, was saving myself from an actual Dragon. It was as close a call as I've ever had, and my survival was due more to dumb luck than skill.

The Dragon was tiny, about the size of a house cat, perfectly camouflaged in the crevice of a rocky trench I was passing through. When it struck, I was just out of range, and that's the only thing that saved me. When I fired I was too close to miss, and it died instantly. I thought it such a lucky break, and left the steaming, stinking carcass patting myself on the back, so proud of my own cleverness. Imagine that.

I performed a sort of solo after-action review, but didn't dwell on it. I was alive, after all. If I had thought it through I would have started running sooner, and a lot faster.

Dragons do not often miss, and I did consider that my luck may have been attributed, at least in part, to the possibility that the creature had been ill or injured. I did not factor in that they vary significantly in size, making it impossible to estimate age. This one could very well have been fully grown - but it wasn't. It was a newborn, and its unskilled attack had been a reflexive act of self-defense.

Less than a day later, a familiar jolt of sickness hit me out of nowhere, alerting me that something was following me - and I was moving well before I ever caught a glimpse of them and their rage. The nausea waxes and wanes, but it's growing steadily stronger.

They damned near had me about a week ago.

I'd been traveling with a group of skulkers. They are the dregs of our herd; mostly made up of the injured or sick, and the scant few old farts who've outlived their utility but somehow manage to stay alive. Although fairly useless, they do occasionally make great camouflage. There were enough in the group to throw the Dragons off, temporarily at least, but I've made good use of the time.

I was off attending to a call of nature when the creatures found the camp, and when the shouting and screaming started, there was no doubt what happened. I didn't even bother to look, too busy trying to run as silently and quickly as possible while pulling up my pants. When I'd reached what I felt was a reasonably safe distance, I pulled my binoculars and got my first good look at my pursuers.

Both were upright, towering high on the rearmost sets of long, multi-jointed legs. Powerful jets of steaming, corrosive liquid streamed from their wide open mouths, coating everything that moved. I got right the hell out of there, stopping only to make sure they weren't following. Each time I looked back, it was worse.

TETHERED

At second glance, everyone caught in the open had been reduced to stumps of running flesh. By the third, most were completely melted, and pooled with the remains of the rest into puddles - like a stew made of flesh, bone, and clothing. Both Dragons were alternately slurping at those puddles and craning their long necks, seeking. Searching for me.

Still, the Dragons themselves are the most beautiful creatures. They are lean, as all land Dragons tend to be, but bigger than any I've seen. Their heads are small compared to their trunks, with slitted eyes that are bright and colorless as crystal. The bodies are stippled and striped in shades of green, camouflaged so perfectly that they would be all but invisible in any sort of vegetation. As they attacked, rows of bioluminescent spots appeared, running down their sides from the jaws to the tips of their tails, pulsing in a rapid linear sequence. It seemed more like magic than a natural phenomenon.

I've stayed alive thus far by being more cunning than other things, but in this race, I'm entirely out of tactics and nearly out of tricks. It's only a matter of time before what luck I have left goes, too. I've always been cautious, but seldom have I been truly afraid. The terror I experienced watching the open-air liquefaction of those skulkers was easily the sharpest emotion I've ever felt. But this is being alive, and I mean to stay that way.

It was quite by luck I happened upon this place, and I had my exit strategy within seconds of the door opening. My cohabiters were my inspiration, in a way. The oldest of the kids is nine, so I think of him as Nine. He's a bright lad. Reminds me a little of myself. He'd been instructed to bolt the door and ensure that nobody unlocked it by accident. Not one of them had to be reminded that monsters are the most dangerous things in the world, but Nine has a presence about him that the others lack. He's made good choices, and I told him so.

Apparently, there were other adults here for a time who *didn't* make good choices, and Nine was the only one who saw what happened to them. The experience did wonders in reinforcing his diligence in securing doors. I like his chances in life, though it makes one wonder why any child, having witnessed such an epic failure, would be so happy to see another grownup, much less invite them in. I guess it was because he could tell that I was even happier to have found them.

We've gotten along fine over the past several days, the kids and I, even though we don't talk as much as they'd like. They watch me constantly, and I smile as reassuringly as I can manage.

From this point on, I can only offer you speculation. My tale is at its end, and one way or another, I will soon be gone. There's no way to know how anything might end, but this is the best-case scenario I can imagine:

Suppose, at this very moment, I catch a glimpse of the tail end of something flashing past one of the windows - or the glint of moonlight reflected in close-set eyes, glittering with cold intelligence. I may hear things scratching about, searching for a way in, trying doors and windows. Maybe I'll get a chill even though it's the middle of summer. It could be all of these things or none. No matter the harbinger, I *know* it's the Dragons because I can feel them coming. The only thing to do is follow the Gospel of the Apocalypse. So...

First, I will grab whichever two children are closest by and toss them out the main door. I may cut one to give the

Dragons an incentive. I'll haul another up one of the ladders and leave it on the roof. The combined noise should be enough to attract anything nearby and keep it busily focused upon those two visible entrances.

The smallest of the kids is a little blonde-haired girl who wears a Minnie Mouse sweatshirt every day. She will accompany me down into the access tunnel below. At its end, there is a small fleet of brand-new armored assault vehicles waiting, already stocked. I'll only need one. Here, Minnie and I will part company.

I toyed with the idea of taking one of them with me, for awhile at least... just in case I need another loud Hail Mary distraction, but by this point any kid would almost certainly be unmanageable. So out the bay door I will go, O Solo Mio, and then drive like a bat out of hell to Annapolis.

Like most rich kids, I know my way around boats. There should be plenty to choose from, wrapped and stored in ridiculously expensive warehouses up and down the Western shore of the Chesapeake. They will have been meticulously cared for and ready to sail.

Those Dragons will never, ever stop chasing me. Biodiversity notwithstanding, I'm betting they are not swimmers. I saw no fins on them, nor webbing or gills, and spitting acid doesn't seem an appropriate trait for aquatic creatures. To get away from them, I'll go as far off the map as I have to. If that means taking a chance with Davey Jones himself, then so be it.

The children don't realize any of this, of course. They're calm and quiet, seen but not heard, as they should be. And me? I'm sitting by the window, cool as Miles Davis, watching the rain slough off the sodden Dred. I don't want to panic my little friends prematurely.

I think of my parents in times like these and smile. Ultimately, the most valuable thing I inherited from them was the realization that success requires sacrifice, dedication, and, if you are aiming really high, a certain ruthlessness.

I can't help but wonder if all of this hasn't been a trial of some sort for me. Perhaps Tether's Seven are still out there, and there is a place waiting for me among them. Maybe membership is not a gift or privilege but something to be earned.

I'd bet anything that the ending is not what you expected... I wish I could see your face right now. Remember the odd sensation I mentioned when I encountered that first nondescript blob of a Monster? I know now that it was the spark of connection. I told you I was made for this world.

Monsters have always been here, didn't you know? They were Us... and sometimes they still are.

Best of luck to you, friend. (You're going to need all you can get). You be sure to keep a weather eye out for Monsters.

P.S. I may still be out there, somewhere, and we may even cross paths someday. Since one can never know when another distraction might be necessary, maybe you better watch out for me, too.

FOUR
IN SEASON

Since time out of mind, Fall has been a living, breathing muse for inspiration. Nothing so moves some artists - be they painters, poets, or musicians - as when the trees begin their slow march to dormancy. Forest canopies become billowing fields of softly swaying fire that run the full October palette of chaotic color; mystical elven greens, simmering oranges, look-at-me yellows, and lifeblood reds.

Wildlife witnesses the change year after year, but how they feel about it, we cannot know, regardless of how evolved they may be. Though the significant decline in human population has transformed many species in astounding ways, they remain unable to speak.

Prey animals, in particular, are more robust than their ancestors. They are faster, stronger, and more intelligent, and in their way, as dangerous as anything that hunts them. In this valley, deer and elk are most abundant. They seem to be everywhere, grazing in lush fields gone hazy with trailers of creeping mist, ears and noses twitching warily in the uncertain wind. There are always predators about.

Wolves, ever-present at all elevations, are a constant threat to all other things, including humans, but by now bears and big cats will have begun migrating down from their summer habitats. Both are more formidable than ever, yet will never be as dangerous as the average human.

There are men nearby even now, closer than any of the animals know. They are gathered together inside of an immense structure, all but invisible except to those who know precisely where it is.

Old-world architecture had devolved, along with most other aspects of society, until function remained the only consideration - that being to pack as many bodies as possible into the smallest available space. Some cities rose so high that they could be seen hundreds of miles away.

It had become so out of perverse necessity perhaps, but most cities sickened until they were eyesores, standing out like lesions on the skin of society and with all the charm of a third-world prison. Cities are a thing of the past and, thankfully, not likely to return.

This dwelling looks as though it might have thrust up out of the Earth herself. It tumbles along the steep, rocky slope of a series of wooded hills, nestled deep in a copse of hardwoods. But for the windows and doors it could be one of Tolkien's fabled Ents, settling in for the long sleep of winter.

Aesthetically, it rises above and beyond most any other human architecture of its time - not an easy achievement by any means - but in function, there is nothing like it anywhere else. It is the First Jæger Lodge, headquarters of the only remaining exclusive society.

There used to be millions of organizations, Clubs, Fellowships, or Orders of one thing or another, and countless diverse groups of humans to fill them. There are no more societies, no special interest groups. No cliques. Only four distinct groups of people remain.

Foremost are the Scions, species Homo superior, who, even with a total population of less than a million people, make up most of the world's population. Jægers, technically a subgroup of the first, make up the second and smallest of the four. The name is derived, appropriately, from an old-world word for hunter.

The third is composed of what remains of Homo sapiens, commonly referred to as the Tribe. They are a resilient people who, if left to their own ends, might eventually reestablish themselves as the apex society. None who belong to that group are tolerated on Scion territory.

The fourth group has no official name. They are primarily indigenous people who for the most part have never been interested in the happenings of the outside world. Some, like the First Nation, have gladly returned to the old ways of their ancestors. Others, like the inhabitants of Sentinel Island, have only ever wanted to be left alone. These are people who have always responded to unwanted visitors with immediate, lethal violence. The Scions wisely opt to leave them be.

Fortunately, the same cannot be said for the Scions, particularly those within the Jæger Lodge. In most settings, they are as sociable and welcoming as any people in history.

The lodge itself is even more impressive within. It is deceptively large, with spacious rooms and a labyrinth of vast, stone-tiled halls that bore deep into the hills. There are multiple kitchens and bakeries, breweries, wine cellars, and distilleries. Somewhere within there is also a medical facility, state-of-the-art but seldom used. Injuries occur now and again, mostly hunting accidents, but sickness of any sort is virtually unheard of. There are also private chambers, many with cleverly hidden overlooks into the forest. Excepting special invitation, they are off-limits to all save the Jægers themselves. It is perhaps the only restriction in all of Scionic society.

Front and center of the lodge lies the Great Hall. It is an enormous, vaulted amphitheater of hardwood beams and fitted stone. Massive hearths blaze at the corners, curtained by waterfalls fed by springs from within the Earth. Towering panels of transparent tungsten make up almost the entire length of the front wall. They are as close to impenetrable as a barrier can be but do not at all hinder the spectacular, crystal-clear view of the valley and the snow-capped mountains that ring it.

The lodge is so quiet that, from the outside, it seems deserted, although nothing could be farther from the truth. It is packed, and well beyond what might be considered safe capacity.

Jægers and their guests find it difficult to move about, but none seem to mind. The lucky ones have secured comfortable, overstuffed leather chairs, which they carefully guard. Most sit in groups at raised tables or are squeezed shoulder-to-shoulder on rough-hewn benches. They drink and banter as they've done for hundreds of years within these very walls, and most would be hard-pressed to choose which of the two activities they favor most.

Something special is happening here today, and the number of non-Jægers is unusually high. Though there are many traditional hunters among the Scion population, lodges are not places they frequent. It's not that they aren't made to feel welcome – no Jæger would dare treat a guest with anything less than absolute courtesy. Those who do not belong to the order just seem to sense that they are out of their element. They are not wrong.

In a far corner of the lodge, a troupe of musicians plays antique electrical string instruments by candlelight, covering a mix of songs dating back to the late twentieth century. The last notes of "Rosanna" wend throughout the crowd, and the finale draws appreciative applause. The susurrus of music, gossip, and laughter mixes with the aromas of food and drink, creating an atmosphere that is heavenly, idyllic, one might even say - right up until the moment the doors explode inwards.

The massive slabs of carved Lignum-Vitae slam back against the walls with enough force to knock the nearest trophy heads askew. Drinks are spilled and tables overturn. Most of the guests are caught entirely by surprise by the sudden disruption. Some few even cry out in panic at the unknown danger. But when most look back on the event, it will not be the commotion but instead the reaction of the Jægers that they will remember most disturbing.

Chair legs scrape in sawdust and slouches and grins vanish as scores of men and women surge to their feet. The motion is instantaneous and organic, like the coordinated murmuration of starlings. It is smooth, fast, efficient, and purposeful as a wolf pack at hunt. Weapons appear as if by magic. Some swing towards the entry, others pivot to cover the remainder of the room.

The Jægers are ready because it is their nature. They've been designed and bred to deal with the unexpected. Biologically speaking, Scions are not even truly "human," and the Jægers even less so. Physical similarities remain, but at the cellular level they would be almost unrecognizable to their forebears.

In the ensuing calamity, it goes largely unnoticed that a handful of the Jægers have not reacted, save for smirks and expressions of long-suffering tolerance. Their complacency borders on nonchalance, though not due to a lack of awareness. They do not respond because each of those few knew the attack was coming long before it arrived.

Chief among the unimpressed is Arlon Hawking. He is seated in his customary place at a small, private bar, somewhat removed from the main, and one of a scant few who has not even troubled himself to turn and look.

A portion of his mind is an autonomous, symbiotic entity that contemporary neurology has dubbed the Harbinger. It is a separate consciousness operating independently of all other neurological processes and whose sole purpose is to protect the host body in which it exists. It is a new and unprecedented trait in the animal kingdom, thus far manifesting only in Jægers. Even the most subtle changes in the outside world had been enough for the Harbinger to nudge Arlon's brain.

First, a brooding scrub jay had called, alarmed despite the safety of her lofty perch. Birds are often better guardians than dogs. When the threat reached an unacceptable level, she took wing. Joined almost immediately in her panicked flight by dozens of others, great and small, the combined wingbeats created small but distinct changes in air pressure that Arlon could sense even through the thick stone wall.

Then, something had caught the attention of the small, local herd of elk and deer. The animals tensed, snorting clouds of steam and nervously stomping the ground, tracking the intrusion as it drew closer to the lodge. Arlon tracked the movement of their eyes and ears just as intently.

Finally, there was an abrupt and profound interval of silence, like the diastolic hush between heartbeats. Something very large had come between the lodge's outer doors and the bluster of the wind.

These indicators notwithstanding, it was mostly instinct which apprised Arlon and the other Jægers of his caliber that what approached was not a serious threat. This conclusion had been communicated via surreptitious nods and knowing looks they'd shared. Very few things could approach a Jæger outpost undetected, and any legitimate threat would have been neutralized long before it reached the lodge - probably without disrupting the festivities.

Arlon sipped his drink and glanced into the mirror at the blazing rectangle of daylight in the doorway behind him and the silhouette of the intruder who now occluded it. A gust of chill wind tore inside, smelling of early snow. Small cyclones of leaves swirled briefly in the wake, curling at the feet of the immense figure that all but extinguished the paling sapphire light of evenfall behind him. The form was distinctly man-shaped and huge, filling the space almost as completely as the doors.

A spatter of multicolored dots instantly appeared upon the target, quickly coalescing into smaller, tighter rings centered on heart and head. There was an instant of tense, deathly silence - broken when someone at the front of the crowd muttered, "Fucking Tyson," the words dripping with exasperation that was shared by all of the regulars in the room. The enormity began to shake with laughter and reached up to lower its hood.

Arlon smiled in spite of himself. *You'd think they'd expect it by now*, he thought. The band, he noted, had remained impressively unruffled by the noisy intrusion of Jæger weaponry – in itself a musical chorus of hums, chirps, and whines that almost belied their lethality. Without missing a beat, they launched into an acoustic version of "Life In The Fast Lane."

Nobody actually fired a weapon. Even the lowest ranking Jæger was too disciplined and well-trained for that, as all who carried implements of death should be. There were weapons in this room that could instantly transform hostile targets into steaming puddles, dust, or clouds of pink vapor. Some fired compressed-energy projectiles which struck with the force of a medieval cannonball and could render a body into a misshapen bag of bone fragments. Others left basically nothing behind save a legacy of poor decision-making on the part of the target.

There were those also, of course, that were designed to incapacitate only, but even the most benign of these would blow a field-fortified intruder right back out the door, likely causing them to soil themselves in the process. *Which would serve them right*, Arlon thought with amusement.

Someone *had* thrown a tomahawk at Gaither once, which had bounced ineffectually off his kinetic armor. It had, most opined, been intended as a joke.

Arlon finished off his drink, which was replaced before he thought to order another. He scratched at his close-cropped auburn beard as he evaluated the disturbance from a tactical standpoint. Strategically, an attack upon the lodge could be balls-out brilliant.

Arlon might consider it if he were of a mind … and if it were currently four hundred years ago. Statistically, an enemy was more likely to be killed by a small asteroid than successfully staging a military assault against Jægers. Even marginally disrupting any part of Scion society would be a feat in itself.

Despite being counterintuitive to the point of idiocy, the tactic of choosing direct frontal assault had somehow proven effective numerous times throughout ancient military history. In almost every other scenario in nature, it was usually suicide. Antelopes did not venture into tall grass looking to gore tigers, and even crocodiles knew better than to push their luck on the hippos' side of the river. Just so, no sane man would attack a Jæger, let alone a lodge full of them. *But it was also the last thing an enemy might expect,* Arlon admitted to himself, *which was why hyenas were able to kill lions.*

The laser sites winked out as quickly as they'd appeared, and hostility gave grudging way to hisses and cursing and grumbles of aggravated relief. There was an air of general confusion among many of the non-Jaegers, which was to be expected. A wave of appreciative whistles and cat-calls followed, then a round of general applause pattered like a sudden rain shower throughout the cavernous hall. Sidearms were returned to leather and lips to drinks.

Gaither Carroway-Tyson stepped inside and kicked the doors closed behind him, gave a slight bow to his audience, then stomped up to join Arlon at the bar. He was careful to deliver a vigorous and entirely unnecessary shoulder bump as he reached for the bucket-sized flagon awaiting him. Cold ale splashed into Arlon's crotch, which he ignored as he studied Gaither in the mirror.

At just over seven feet, the man was almost as large as the polar bear whose fur trimmed out the magnificent hunting leathers he wore. It was a matter of local legend and historical record that Gait had killed that monstrous ursa with a spear. In another day and age, the claim would have been instantly and rightly denounced as excrement, except the event had been captured perfectly by one of the small fleets of shadow drones that accompanied Jægers whenever and wherever they hunted.

Based on the looks Gaither was getting from others around them, Arlon knew he wasn't alone in wondering what the creature must have thought when it saw Gait materialize out of the blizzard like a wraith. Probably the bear equivalent of *Would you look at this shit?* It was unlikely that the beast had ever seen a human before, but that would have been inconsequential. Nothing killed bears on land and in their own territory except bigger bears. Anything smaller was prey, and prey was supposed to flee.

But instead of running or freezing in terror, the strange animal – less than a quarter of the bear's weight – had attacked.

Gaither was fortunate that he hadn't instead stumbled upon one of the genetically resurrected short-faced bears that now inhabited the remotest corners of the continent. A game hunter would have slightly better odds of trying to kill an earthquake. Arlon eyed him. He gave it fifty-fifty odds that Gaither might give it a shot anyway. The man was by no means a fool, but he was still Gaither and, therefore, likely to do just about anything.

The stool creaked under Gaither's weight as he drained his first drink and gestured for another. This he downed in slower, more appreciative gulps, then belched in a manner that seemed inappropriate for a man with an IQ so high that it couldn't be quantified. He waved for a third, then paused, snuffling at the air. He leaned in until his nose almost touched the faded leather beanie Arlon wore. "It smells like deep-fried ass in here." He rumbled. "Is that your breath, or did someone shit in your hat?"

Arlon waited for Gaither to tip his vessel before he replied. "Neither, actually. Your sister was just here dancing on the bar again... naked as usual. I'm sure I speak for everyone when I say thanks for airing the place out."

There was a chorus of laughter from those within earshot as the other man snorted, coughing on a mouthful of dark mead. A hand roughly the size of a catcher's mitt walloped Arlon on the back.

"Well played, *sadiqi*." He belched again. "But you're sweeter on her than you are full of shit, and that's saying something." He gestured vaguely at the room. "Every man in this place would give an eyeball to get next to Laney, and you know it." Arlon noticed a heavily tattooed, silver-haired Jæger farther down the bar, speculatively nodding his assent to nobody in general, the sub-dermal Mosaic markings on his arms pulsing in rhythm with the music.

Gaither was wasting no time in catching up in his drinking, and when half of the big man's mead was down the hatch, Arlon spoke again. "From what I understand, lots of guys have thrown balls her way, often and regularly, and I'm not talking about their eyes." He shrugged theatrically. "All I'd have to throw away would be sobriety, good judgment, and standards."

This time, the mead got some distance, spraying out over the bar and earning a scowl from the keep, who'd not managed to entirely avoid the shower.

Gaither eventually choked his composure back into place and gave Arlon an affectionate nudge that would have knocked a smaller, weaker man to the floor. "Like you'd ever be sober." He finally managed, wiping his watering eyes on his sleeve.

Arlon swirled his drink and grinned in smug self-satisfaction as his best friend dealt with the searing fire in his sinuses. But Gait was right. Arlon loved Elayne from the moment they met, and he knew how lucky he was. Some people went their whole lives without ever realizing what it was to love and be loved in return.

He'd remember it until his dying day. She'd appeared from behind an enormous oak that rose from the courtyard of her family's estate. It had been like unexpectedly crossing the path of a brindle panther - her eyes like ice on fire and focused on him with an intensity that only predators can manage. Her mouth had twitched into the quirky grin he'd grown to know so well, and then, without so much as a hello or word of warning, she'd pounced on him.

Arlon's father had laughed himself almost sick as they tussled, she trying her best to manipulate him into position to choke him out while he struggled to counter. He'd managed to not get strangled, but only just. It seemed odd to Arlon sometimes that love could take its first breath like that, yet here they were all these long years later.

Elayne loved him, too, in her way. Or so he believed. You couldn't ever be sure of another person's true feelings. Sure, people had been able to communicate without words for going on nearly three centuries, but even the most advanced telepathic communication had limitations. The nuance of feeling was often lost in translation. The difference was like comparing black-and-white technical manuals to poetry written in flowing, gold-leaf calligraphy.

For his part, Arlon was quite happy with their relationship. He reckoned that what they had in each other was more than what most couples enjoyed, and that was more than enough. They shared passion for everything that mattered, yet were different enough to have remained exciting and surprising to one another for over eighty years. She wasn't the type to ever ask him to justify his feelings for her, but he'd once told her, long ago, that he never had to pretend to be interested in her. She'd kissed him and told him it was the best compliment she'd ever received.

For him, the best thing was that they could always make one another laugh, and he valued their wealth of private jokes more than anything he could think of. Other elements of a relationship came and went, but it took something special to want to grow old with another person ... especially considering how long that could be. Their families had been tied together for centuries, and if things continued to go well, they'd spent several more together. Once merely a concept of romantic poetry and song, it wasn't out of the realm of possibility to say that they could well end up together forever. In case of accidental death, all Scions had their consciousness safely downloaded, and printing a new body was as easy as buying a new pair of hunting boots.

They did everything together, including hunting, and it was in equal parts chilling and arousing to watch. Arlon could picture her face clearly, her gaze like liquid nitrogen as she stalked and tracked, a huntress wholly in her element. She moved with the speed and grace of a lioness, remorselessly taking down prey with any weapon you cared to name – or none at all. A heat washed over him that had nothing to do with drink. Nothing was sexier than a woman who could hunt, and Laney was one of the best he'd ever known. She was out there somewhere right now, hunting alone. He glanced out the window into the shadowy forest, a slow grin spreading across his face.

The average person could be taught the basics of practically any skill, but in Arlon's long experience, it was quite rare to be born with the instincts and innate abilities to be the thing you wanted most to be, even among the Scions.

Despite having been born without a Harbinger, she was a better killer than Gaither or any of her other siblings... and better than Arlon himself. Both men were well aware of this fact. It wasn't discussed.

Reluctance to acknowledge her prowess was in no way a sex issue. It was just part of the game. Braggadocio among outdoor sportsmen was an art unto itself, shaped and honed by its practitioners since the beginning of time. Hunters, in particular, were not known for humility - regardless of gender - and never had been.

They were surpassed in this regard only by fishermen, if only by a hair. The unusual longevity of Earth's prevailing people made them far more adept at this wry, ageless art than their predecessors could've dreamed.

The most accomplished were poet-assassins who wielded verbal abuse like a rapier, slashing and piercing those who, in the main, they were most fond of. There did not need to be a special reason to unleash the hounds of humiliation, however there *were* occasions during which it was expected. It just so happened to be the case this very afternoon and the reason Gaither looked fit to burst.

It was a testament to her independence that Elayne was not present for the shenanigans currently underway, and more than a little ironic considering that she'd played such a large part in putting him in the situation he was in.

TETHERED

Arlon nursed his drink as long as etiquette allowed, then sighed, finally acknowledging Gaither's impatient expression in the mirror. "How'd you make out today, mudwhistle?"

Gaither slapped his slab of a palm on the bar top. "So glad you asked, you sandbagging dingleberry!"

Prick doesn't even have the good grace to sound nonchalant, Arlon thought with an amused scowl.

Weeks earlier, Arlon had been gifted a pass to hunt the Gaia Rout, arguably the most coveted sport hunt in the world due to its rarity. The last one, attended by his father, had occurred more than forty years ago.

There had been many congratulations, of course, all of which had promptly degraded into a stiff bout of metaphorical dick-measuring. The unanimous, alcohol-fueled consensus was that only a hunter of legendary prowess was worthy of such a prize, regardless of how they'd come by it.

Naturally, a heated debate followed about who might fall into such a narrow, prestigious category. Gallons of beer, wine, and ale flowed, prompting filibusters of bragging and apelike chest-beating the likes of which even the old-timers couldn't recall. Elayne had been there, grinning wickedly throughout the entire process, fanning the flames with well-timed barbs and insults and thoroughly enjoying both men's obvious apprehension that she'd take a side, or worse - insist on being included in the competition.

Fortunately for both of them, Elayne preferred to hunt alone, and the only benchmarks she recognized were those she set for herself.

In the wee hours of that fateful morning, it was ultimately decided that whomsoever shall have the most bountiful hunt on the final day of the regular fall season would take possession of the pass. The fact that it was Arlon's to begin with somehow never factored into the equation.

Today was judgment day, with the official judging to be done an hour before sunset. This would be performed by eleven of the eldest members of this most esteemed club - the Jæger equivalent of Mensa - but with all the requisite favoritism and bias one expected from a group of consummate bullshit artists.

Arlon had finished early, and his lot was already weighed, inspected, and documented. Fortune smiled upon him, and it had been one of the best hunts of his life. The judges had been duly impressed, and he'd considered himself unbeatable. Now, the haughty look on Gaither's ruddy, windburned face was making him unsure. The behemoth was by no means above making false claims, but he seemed far too confident for Arlon's comfort.

The eldest son of the Carroway-Tyson clan paused until every ear was tuned and waiting. Finally, he winked and grinned. "I had the best hunt of my life."

Arlon lifted his drink to a chorus of excited whispers that rose all around. "As did I, mighty warrior." he replied, draining the last of his mug. He placed it on the bar top, slapped his thigh, and stood. "Welp." he sneered, turning to the doors. "You know what they used to say about money and bullshit."

There was a great scuffle as the throng came to its feet and migrated to the exits. A great many bets were being placed, both official and not, and the tension was palpable as they filed out into the glory of October's perfection. Money, heirloom weapons, and other treasured things would change hands this day. Almost as valuable would be the bragging rights that came with supporting the winning side.

Gait was already actively re-living the details of his hunt, his bold claims borne upon majestic white clouds of breath as he embellished the bordering-on-impossible conditions he'd had to overcome. It was shaping up to be a true *"No shit, there I was..."* presentation. The audience crowded him so as not to miss a detail, frosty leaves crunching beneath their feet. The distant mountaintops rose before them in Appaloosa-patterned patches of evergreen and snow.

Arlon stooped and grabbed a small twig off the ground and began to absently pick at his teeth as he listened to Gait blather on. *Let him,* he thought. All the better when Arlon claimed victory. He began to mull over the highlights of his own hunt, his thoughts straying into the feral poetry of it.

Hunting was not about the act of killing for its own sake. In fact, the very thought was distasteful enough that Arlon frowned. Several of his comrades nearby took note and scanned the wood line, wondering what might be bothering him.

A successful hunt was a melding of art, science, and spirituality. It required dedication. Stalking and tracking demanded high levels of physical stamina and mental discipline, and waiting for prey could be even more so. Hunters were obligated to spend long periods absolutely still, scanning the environment for the barest movement that might give away the location of prey, or worse, their own position.

For Arlon, a successful kill was a requisite, and should never require more than one shot. There was a particular mindset required to make an ethical kill. One must regulate their emotions, breathing, and thoughts into a state of zen-like calm before squeezing a trigger or loosing an arrow.

No single group in man's history knew the thrill of the hunt better than the Jægers, but they were as different as snowflakes in their methods and reasoning. Arlon took time for introspection at the beginning and end of every hunt. It wasn't a prayer, per se, but close enough.

Religion had died with the old world, finally dismissed as the useless method of manipulation it had always been. Homo sapiens could never seem to get enough of its ridiculous, illogical minutiae and had jumped from one discipline to another throughout their entire existence – not that it was necessarily their fault. Translation of multiple dead languages definitively established that man had been designed and bred to serve. All the more reason that no Scion would dream of entertaining so much as a paragraph of any holy text, except perhaps as a source of amusement.

Hunting, on the other hand, was intrinsic to almost every creature to ever live on Earth. Food was second on the list of prime necessities for humans, right between water and shelter, and that made the rituals of acquiring it more spiritual than any religious rite could hope to be. It was an intimate, respectful acknowledgment of the kinship shared by all life, Arlon believed. That was why hunting culture had endured and continued to evolve, and always must. Outside biological necessity, hunting was also the Jægers' primary function. They protected and maintained the harmony that so much blood had been shed to achieve.

The Hawkings and Caraway-Tysons were Consiglieri, direct descendants of the founding members of the First Council – the entity responsible for saving planet Earth. They were also among the few bloodlines that successfully coexisted with their Harbingers.

Arlon was ever aware of his own - a sentinel that never slept. It was like seeing the world with two sets of eyes at all times. Right now, Arlon saw his friends, neighbors, and fellow hunters all around, the nearby woods and the skies above, but his Harbinger was aware of things that no ordinary human could.

If Arlon desired it, it could tell him the exact temperature and humidity, wind speed and direction, and the likelihood of bad weather. It knew the species of all wildlife in the immediate area, even approximating the number and sex of the animals in each pack or herd.

The Harbinger knew how those around him were feeling at any given moment based on their body language, translating a person's slightest micro-expression into a broadcast of intent. It was difficult to lie to a Jæger or deceive them in any way... and nearly impossible to attack one with any hope of surviving the encounter. If only the previous civilization of man had been so intuitive, they might have persevered, but their own shortcomings and the actions of the First Council had assured otherwise.

It all began with those founders of the Tether Corporation, who had started with a dream of changing the world. None of them could have known that their impact on the course of humanity would be more significant than the reign of Genghis Khan, whose conquest had literally changed the climate of the entire planet. Did they know from the start that they would be obligated to eventually rule the world as a whole? There was no reason to believe that the Council's charter would have included world domination as one of its primary objectives, although even Arlon would admit that the histories were vague on certain aspects of Tether's beginnings.

Global conquest had been attempted countless times. Historians uniformly judged such campaigns to be philosophically wrong, morally and ethically evil, and ultimately an unattainable ambition. They had no reason to think otherwise, for none had ever succeeded. Each attempt left indelible marks on humanity. Some proved ultimately beneficial, bringing technology, prosperity, and an overall higher quality of life to the conquered, but never without leaving ugly scars on societies that never completely healed.

The commonality was that no matter how profound or enduring the conquest, one of two things inevitably occurred. Either somebody came along with a bigger stick, or the reigning empire collapsed under the weight of its own folly.

The only point upon which all scholars had always agreed was that total, permanent conquest would never be possible. But if history ever proved anything, it's that nothing is impossible. The First Council would succeed where all others had failed – and had done so without a single soldier at their command. This time, instead of unleashing the dogs of war and ushering in yet another era of hell on Earth, the Consiglieri decided to try a different approach.

The Council began Tether Industries as a humble biotech startup, a mere handful of men and women determined to provide diversified philanthropic solutions for the betterment of all mankind. In short, Tether's mission was to solve the world's unsolvable issues. The Corporate world collectively scoffed at this... at least until Tether began succeeding. Virtually everything they attempted, they accomplished, and quickly came to be regarded as a lifeline for people worldwide.

They grew carefully, wisely limiting interference despite the sudden clamor from outside interests to expand. Financial suitors were carefully vetted, and very few would meet Tether's ethical standards. Eventually, they did find investors who shared their core values – which were more than simply words to Tether's leadership. While their growth wasn't rapid, it was rock solid. Tether never dared get remotely close to relinquishing control, though once public, the company made its shareholders wealthy beyond their wildest dreams.

Tether would eventually contribute trillions of dollars to a host of projects. Before the end of their first decade in existence, they virtually eliminated childhood starvation. They became the first and only organization in history to actually cure diseases without creating addiction or financially bleeding the sick into poverty to do so.

By the time Tether celebrated its thirtieth anniversary, it had become the wealthiest organization in human history, surpassing Microsoft, Apple, and Amazon combined. The Consiglieri believed they'd reached a level that would allow them to finally focus their considerable intellect, resources, and standing on the world political stage to achieve their ultimate goal: establishing total and lasting world peace.

It was when the Council began shopping this proposal to world leadership that they got their first glimpse into the inconceivable depths of absolute power and corruption.

They'd genuinely believed that a higher standard of decency existed, and it simply wasn't true of the creatures with whom they'd sought to reason. They soon discovered, to their profound disgust and horror, that there were no lengths to which people would not go to seize and retain control.

Scions who made a study of the events considered the First Council to be as naive as they were decent, which only made their success all the more impressive. Time and again they pleaded their case, each time finding themselves batting against a glass ceiling. Publicly, Tether was profusely thanked and lauded for all their good works and assured that their peace initiative would be taken under the most serious consideration. But behind closed doors, it was an entirely different story.

A particularly ugly reality was that leaders of even the world's most impoverished and beaten-down nations had their country's affairs precisely as they wanted them. They had no intention of conceding an iota of power or personal wealth, regardless of how beneficial it might be for their people. In some cases, they didn't even consider their citizens to be the same species of human beings, barely better than chattel. If only they could have foreseen the irony.

The Council had never been infected by greed. It's impossible for that sin to coexist with the genuine desire to do good. Not one man or woman among them could even comprehend what a corrosive thing it was to be addicted to power for its own sake. The more they learned, the more sickened and frustrated they became until finally, out of frustration, the Council began to expose the actions of the corrupt to the world at large.

Here, the cabal that truly ran the world made themselves known, and Tether would soon come to learn a few subtle but important lessons. Foremost among them was that limitless power was a real thing.

Where once their efforts had been met with obstruction and misdirection, Tether now encountered solid walls and active resistance. It began to experience sanctions and fines instead of support. Tether's people were no longer welcome in places that needed them the most.

Their engineering, medical, and field security operators had regularly dealt with militias and guerrilla forces; people with whom they could reason more often than not. Now, it was the host nation's armed forces that they found themselves facing. Equipment and supplies would be confiscated or destroyed, followed by an armed expulsion of Tether's people and a stern warning to not return. One of the groups discovered sneaking back over the border was never seen again. The people they'd been aiding were murdered, and their villages razed to the ground.

The blame for these tragedies was hung around Tether's neck, and local and national media made the false allegations of Tether's malfeasance stick. Back home, the Council suddenly found themselves under the scrutiny of the IRS and other foreign bodies, with no justification whatsoever. Almost all of their philanthropic work was halted pending investigation of "financial irresponsibilities" and "alleged connection to atrocities."

Still, despite the threat, the Council persisted. It was made known to the Council that if Tether persisted in interfering in the affairs of other governments, there were leaders who could and would simply ensure there would be no people to help. One President-Dictator of a small African country had explained matter-of-factly to Robert Carroway that most of the inhabitants of his country weren't of his tribe. Therefore, they were his property... to be used, abused, or disposed of as he saw fit. Furthermore, anyone wearing the Tether logo found in his country and working counter to his interests would likewise be considered his property and dealt with accordingly.

Still, the Council wanted to help - an exercise in futility when trying to play by rules that did not exist. They made every attempt to comply with all of the bullshit sanctions and obstacles and get back to the work to which they were so committed. But those who held the strings decided it was time to make an example for other crusaders who might consider following in Tether's footsteps. Politics was the God of currency, and avarice was His greasy, black blood.

For every step forward, Tether was often forced to take a dozen back. In the vacuum of their humanitarian aid, conditions in many places worldwide deteriorated. For a time, more wars were being simultaneously fought on Earth than ever before in history. Red dots on military maps depicting civilian deaths made it look as though the planet was dying of smallpox.

Frustration is corrosive to the soul, and it festered in the minds of the Founders like cancer. They were, above all, good men and women who were resolute in their determination to make a difference, but even the kindest and most generous people have limits. It was inevitable that something would break, and when it did, the Council became something Other. Few things are more dangerous than the rage of peaceful men.

The Consiglieri unanimously decided that as far as the world's fate was concerned, they would no longer require nor seek approval. It was clear to anyone with eyes that the world was on a collision course, which could not be allowed. Any and all means necessary to alter that course were now on the table. They quietly began to lay the groundwork for what would come to be known as the Transition.

Arlon believed there was never a doubt they would succeed, but he often wondered how they'd felt as the necessary courses of action became clear. The process itself was meticulously documented, but as to the emotional cost, who could ever know without having been there in person? Irregardless of their feelings, nobody could argue that the architects were infinitely qualified.

First, their motives were altruistic. Scions, in general, never sought undue wealth or power. They'd always been genetically predisposed to preserve and protect, and these tendencies remained potent in the blood lines of the descendants of the original Consiglieri.

Second, they were more than sufficiently motivated. The Transition, by any other name, was probably always inevitable, the Jæger mused, but the personal nature of the attacks on the Consiglieri had been like gas on an open fire. The financial abuse had been vicious, and the casual arrogance and disregard with which they'd been dismissed even worse. But it was the extent to which the world was being mismanaged by those in power - like stupid children playing with their fathers' guns - that ultimately prompted them into action. It is said that hell hath no fury like a woman scorned, but that sentiment applies to anyone if they are pushed too far.

Last, and most importantly, they were the smartest people ever to exist.

With a path now illuminated before them, Tether recovered quickly. They made a great show of compliance and were finally accepted back into the fold, where they progressed in leaps and bounds. If anything, they advanced faster and more efficiently than ever before. And the things they created...

Tether had worked out the host of problems associated with the development of a successful AI decades prior while even the most technologically advanced governments were still fumbling. It was to be the first and most significant of accomplishments that the Consiglieri would neglect to share with the worldwide scientific community.

They were the first to successfully harvest dark matter, which, when coupled with the stabilization of Element-15, fathered zero-point energy machines. These allowed for gravity nullification - or levitation - and entire new families of vehicles and weapon systems. The least powerful of the latter were focused-energy weapons that virtually every Scion in the civilized world carried. Visible or not, all of the folks chatting across the field toward Gaither's Buteo were armed with one version or another.

Some of their discoveries had been accidental, and quite beyond the reckoning of almost anyone outside the organization. The Tether Applied Physics people laid the groundwork for wormhole mapping, holographic cloaking, and a score of other wonders that would eventually be utilized in achieving the changes the Council desired.

But their most remarkable feat by far would be the ability to protect their discoveries. Modern-day historians greatly emphasized the level of loyalty shared by the original founding families. It made infiltration - corporate, governmental, or otherwise, absolutely impossible.

It was not a historian but a famous twentieth-century comedian who'd probably summed it up best when he said, *"You could take over the world with five loyal friends."* He could never have known how right he was.

If there had been outsiders intelligent enough to grasp the bare edges of these concepts, they would not have needed Tether, and therein did their downfall lay. Outwardly, the

Council continued to show its belly to the established powers. This act of compliance, coupled with their track record of getting results where all others typically failed, made Tether the golden child of all government contractors. The Council's inner circle gained unprecedented access to the highest levels of intelligence information. A select few were read-in on Projects that were beyond "black." Some were so secret that they had no classification, and the President of the United States himself had no knowledge of them.

Governments, institutions of faith, and corporations could not be trusted. Their time was past. So it was that only the least significant of Tether's innovations would ever make it into the incompetent hands of bureaucrats. Still, caution was in order.

Tether was now dealing with the people at the absolute top of the pyramid of power. The Consiglieri thought they'd already been horrified at the control exercised upon the world populace. They'd had no idea. It had seemed impossible that there could be people worse than those they'd already encountered - until it became necessary to do business with the Military Industrial Complex.

It turned out that the world was under the near absolute control of this pack of unaccountably wealthy sociopaths. The private journals of the Council describe them as possibly the most vile and indiscriminate scum to have ever existed. In his personal journal, Arlon's great-grandfather had written: *"These creatures have less concern for human life than most people have for the dirt beneath their feet. As long as such a human condition exists, there can never be peace."*

More than anything, it would be this proximity that triggered the Consiglieri to pursue such dramatic and violent solutions. Those in power had always possessed the financial resources to end all of mankind's woes. They could have put a halt to war with an email. Not only were they not worthy to lead… they were not worthy of being termed human.

But how far would an entity have to go to fix things? The answer was unanimous and irrefutable: *As far as necessary*. And it would not be subtle or pleasant. Lasting peace could not be negotiated into existence. There was no single example of its occurrence in all recorded human history. Peace had only ever been rented, for it was always temporary. But it *had to* happen. Sometimes, a healer must sacrifice a limb to save a patient, and so would it be with Earth.

Primary among their beliefs was a fundamental notion that without a healthy planet upon which to live, all other considerations were irrelevant. The common man could never be relied upon to remedy widescale pollution. Most were destitute. Before Tether's interventions, anywhere between twenty and twenty-five thousand thousand children were dying from starvation every single day, and it was happening on a planet full of food. In the most repressed societies, women couldn't summon up enough hope to name their newborns, knowing they were unlikely to live long enough to ever hear the love in a mother's voice.

People who existed in such a state could not be expected to give a shit that the governments of most third-world countries were dumping millions of tons of garbage into the planet's oceans annually. It was ridiculous to expect such a thing from anyone struggling just to survive.

People in First-World countries protested these things regularly, providing that it did not negatively affect their lifestyle. They raged against fossil fuels while holding phones made of petroleum products, stomped their feet wearing shoes made of petroleum products, and drove and flew to organized protests in vehicles and aircraft that ran on petroleum products.

"...easily the fastest one I've ever hunted." Gaither's voice carried back to Arlon from somewhere up ahead. He shook his head and grinned. It felt good that a world now existed where the best in mankind had persevered. Humanity wasn't perfect. Never had been and never would be. But it was in harmony, and that was something.

It was an exceptionally beautiful day. There wasn't a river or lake that wasn't clean enough to drink from. There were no piles of trash or toxic waste, nor a single drop of poison in any ocean or sea. The only thing that would have made it better was Laney's presence.

The Transition had made all of this possible. It was a masterpiece in theory and a thing of beautiful simplicity in practice, as all best-laid plans tend to be, but there had been endless questions that needed to be fielded. Among the most important was how to go about it.

Divine imperative was out of the question and not even considered. By this time, subjugation through superstition had ceased to be a viable option for accomplishing anything. The last Big Gods were in their death throes, having been dragged into the revelatory dawn of the Age of Information. Spirituality was as strong as ever, but it would have been impossible to fool people en mass with preposterous threats of heavenly punishment that could not be enforced. Not that any among the Council would ever have stooped to such primitive means.

Neither was all-out global war discussed. It is always crude and inhumane, not to mention the inevitable collateral environmental damage that was counter to their every goal.

The Consiglieri considered it to be utterly beneath them on every level.

Most importantly, when Tether struck there could be a zero percent possibility of large-scale retaliation. There is art in subtlety, and the Council took it as somewhat of a challenge to elicit their desired changes with the precision of an atomic clock.

They started with two fundamentals. First was the indisputable fact, known to all serious students of history, that the most powerful empires must fall from within. Second, in the end, that power lies in the will of the masses. Willing compliance of the human race was essential for success and far easier to gain than with forcible coercion. Luckily, the Council had been unwittingly handed an unexpected and priceless gift that radically expedited their plans. It was a digital file labeled "Omelette."

The information was believed to have been destroyed but instead somehow lost by the NSA - only to be rediscovered among the terabytes of digital information accessible to Tether's people. It was undoubtedly a bureaucratic blunder, a bit of misappropriated information that survived to become another ghost in the machine.

Though seemingly innocuous in name, it pinged the curiosity of the head of Tether's genetic research department. She is quoted in Tether's historical archives, describing its contents "as diabolical as it was convenient."

Omelette was nothing less than a detailed account of the genetic manipulation of virtually every person in the civilized world. The process dated back to the mid-1950s, well before any Consiglieri were even born.

The method was invisible, implemented via gene drives. It is unlikely that even one percent of people in the mid-nineteenth century had the faintest idea of the existence of deoxyribonucleic acid, much less its significance. But in the centuries to follow, DNA would be found useful in a great many ways. Most of these had been intended to be beneficial to the betterment of mankind. Certainly, it had begun that way.

Regrettably, it was also discovered that it could be without equal as a conditioning tool, and developed in that regard more efficiently than anyone suspected.

Desirable traits like submission and compliance were cultivated throughout several generations to counteract awareness and independent thought. The DNA alterations were so insignificant that they would virtually never be discovered, at least not until it was too late. All that was required was for the drives to be introduced into the human body. The delivery systems were obvious and simple to manipulate. Food. Water. Medicine. Things that people would always need.

The food industry was already rapidly moving towards processing and preserving for commercial purposes, and there was never a time when Pharma wasn't corrupt, so it was no trouble whatsoever for the newly formed Food and Drug Administration to get what they wanted into the people they wanted it in. It was all unethical as hell, but ethics were never much of a concern for the powerful - and even less so for the greedy.

Arlon wondered if, even if some random person had ever caught wind of the plot, would anyone have even believed them? It was unlikely, never in a world where people still believed that their governments would never do something so heinous as loading children onto trains bound for ovens. They'd never allow the water supplies of entire towns to be poisoned, even generations after the offending corporations were exposed. *No, sir, not the guy I voted for!* Somebody would have to be crazy to even suggest that a government would allow such things to occur, let alone be the perpetrators.

But there wasn't anything a government wouldn't do, and by the beginning of the twenty-first century, the effects began to become horrifically apparent.

Once embedded at the genetic level, a behavior can never be removed or overcome, at least not in time to make a difference. It was a large part of why Scions, and Jægers in particular, held to the custom of eating only what they killed themselves. *Well,* Arlon amended with grim humor, *most things anyway.*

The gaggle of Scions was crossing the broad, shallow creek that skirted the valley. Arlon ventured upstream and bent to scoop a few handfuls of the frigid water. The shock radiated from his stomach to the tips of his fingers and toes. It was no wonder, he thought, that so many religious rituals involved baptisms of one sort or another. Water was life.

The Council ultimately decided that the power structures must be weakened, thereby shifting the focus of all scrutiny away from Tether. And what more useful or ironic weapon could there be to destroy the corrupt but corruption? None would realize their favored weapon was being used against them before the blade was twisted. And so they began to gather unto themselves the pieces and place them about the board.

Both Church and State had to fall, and the best way to do that was to turn them against one another. There were plenty of financial ties to exploit, but the strongest bond between them was the copious amount of filthy skeletons in their closets. Those who dwelt in the high houses of power on both sides invariably happened to be practitioners of all manner of predation, and it had been the case long before the first religious texts or political documents had ever been written. If the true extent of even the least of their despicable acts were ever brought to light, they'd all be done for.

There had always been an uneasy sharing of power between the two factions, the main benefit being immunity from prosecution. One hand had always washed the blood and filth from the other, to a certain extent, but either would turn on the other faster than someone could say 'amen' if it served them. The Council had counted on this and was not disappointed.

The Consiglieri first approached the Churches. Emotional manipulation was almost as powerful a tool as genetic, and no group had ever been better at it than holy men. There was no small amount of irony in the ease with which they'd been recruited. The emissaries of the Consiglieri quietly reached out to those most high in the holy hierarchies, hinting that a great change was coming and that right soon. If this great and glorious Transition was to succeed, it would be best if it had the consent and support of the people. And who better to guide during difficult times than men of faith? Naturally, it must be held in the utmost secrecy from the bungling of the growing World Order Government. They were godless people, after all, who would do anything to prevent peace. Just look at what they were doing to the world.

Predictably, the representatives of all major religions could not have agreed more, and unanimously declared that they would *absolutely* support any and all of Tether's efforts in implementing the Transition. Anything to stay in control.

Elayne once commented that it must have been especially pleasurable to watch the gold-festooned heads of the fathers of faith roll into the gutters. She hoped that not a single private jet purchased in the name of God had made it into international airspace when they attempted to escape. Most Scions agreed, considering that what had really sealed the deal with the self-appointed representatives of the gods was the ironclad assurance that their multitude of dirty secrets would be kept and certain unsavory practices allowed to continue unabated. When that particular line was cast, they'd practically swallowed the hook.

Whenever discussing this topic, Gaither would generally scowl and interject "*pieces of shit.*" Like a fart in a church, it wasn't a particularly flowery statement, but just as profound. People in today's world were comfortable calling things as they saw them. Arlon could scarcely imagine the disgust the men and women of the Council must have experienced even suggesting such concessions, regardless of the fact that they would never happen. When all was said and done, however, it was probably cleaner than how dealing with the governments made them feel.Attaining the State's cooperation was straightforward. The overwhelming majority of career politicians have always proven inept and power-hungry in almost equal measure. When given the same pitch as that delivered to the Churches, most politicians they approached needed no convincing whatsoever. They were always poised to finally grind all opposition into the dirt if it would increase their own power and influence.

Here, the Council was aided unexpectedly by the social media revolution. Destined from the start to be a game-changer, countless social media venues and platforms were born faster than feral piglets... and proved infinitely more destructive. While most amounted to nothing more than brown skid marks on the fabric of social interaction, even the meanest of them provided an opportunity for disruption.

The phenomenon, once supercharged by Tether's own superior version of AI, swept the world like a digital shitstorm throughout the entire twenty-first century.

The power lay in that everyone suddenly had a voice, even those who'd always been considered lowest in the social hierarchy. Anybody could speak on any issue with little or no danger of retribution. The most ridiculous, insignificant, or dangerous opinions could take root and affect people's lives, whether the consequences landed right down the street or half a world away. This aberration spread like fire in a field, polarizing and destabilizing first-world societies at a level beyond the wildest imagining.

When the potential of social media as a weapon became apparent, breathtaking sums of money were spent by the Church, the State, and the almighty Corporations alike. Distracted humans were even easier to manipulate, and the Council's social media wizards knew that better than any government, Church, or corporation could dream. Tether's AI bots set about transforming distraction into an art form.

The media could have helped to turn things around and shed some much-needed light on what was being done, but trustworthy journalism was defunct. Once an example to an entire world of people, American mainstream media was reduced to less than a shadow of its former greatness. Its pure practitioners had long since been cast out or cannibalized. Those that remained had been all too willing to be bought -

and there is nothing more obedient than a thing that sells itself into slavery.

It was a chaotic time, but so far as the architects of the Transition were concerned, things were going exactly as planned. The Council's people worked in tandem with all three heads of the great hydra, allowing the fires of misinformation to rage, and rage it did for the better part of four decades. Then - slowly, surely, and inevitably - Tether's PR people began subtly turning the tide, pitting each against the others.

The propagandists of each faction began to receive new marching orders, and they were used to doing as they were told. Their masters, true to form, paid little attention. Their focus remained split, as always, between increasing their own wealth and power and staying ahead of the others. Historians agree, however, that even if those in power had been more diligent, it would not have mattered. They were helpless as newborn kittens to what was coming their way.

For what amounted to the course of an entire lifetime for some people, the Council had been monitoring the spread of the socially transmitted disease of misinformation - and specifically its effect upon the peoples of the most technologically advanced societies. It is one thing to recognize what a people desire and quite another to convince them of what those things ought to be. Simply put, the Council persuaded hundreds of millions of people to disable the very means that sustained their social culture.

In terms of establishing control, this non-invasive behavioral modification proved more effective than any other means to have ever existed. It amplified desire, creating unreasonable cravings for not only the material, but also distraction and personal validation. Tether ensured those cravings were well fed, cultivating a near-fanatical desire for approval in the most fortunate and pampered humans who'd ever lived.

It was a monumental achievement, although something curious and unanticipated arose from this aspect of the operation. It was evident in all Scions on Earth to this very day. In the years leading up to the Transition, a small but growing number of people had begun developing an intense aversion to the intervention and overstepping of governments, religions, and corporations. They distrusted the accelerated evolution of technology, and particularly avoided social media like a plague. For all intents and purposes they became invisible, eschewing society and choosing to live apart. It was such a small number of people that they barely showed up as a metric.

In most social circles they were viewed as unstable. Conspiracy theorists. Doomsday preppers. Militiamen. Extremists all. It's fair to say that an infinitesimal percentage of some of those folks were definitely these things, but regardless of the reason for choosing a life on the outskirts they all had one crucial thing in common: They were paying attention to things that most others did not. For a time, they became the most carefully monitored people in history.

It was a real challenge, even for the powerful Tether algorithms tasked with locating them. Nothing is more troublesome to surveil than a man who believes he's being watched. While Tether never had an actual tactical element, they were obligated to make use of satellite and drone surveillance to keep tabs on as many of those outliers as possible. It was critical that they continued to ignore what was happening in the world they'd chosen to abandon. The Council had no illusions as to what would transpire should even the slightest hint of the Transition somehow become known to these people of surprising means and motivations. They were not a group who were likely to simply voice their outrage on their favorite social media platform that Tether was planning on killing almost every man, woman, and child on planet Earth.

Would these ancestors of the Scions have found it ironic that it was their lack of tribal inclinations and social imperatives that distinguished them as shapers of society to come? Arlon wondered. The more pertinent question was: Would they have fought alongside their brothers and sisters, had they known what was to come, or abandoned them to their fate? Arlon was sure the Consiglieri must have considered it.

Nobody would ever know, for the end of things had already reached the point of no return. But for those scattered few, society was descending into complete chaos, and nobody could be sure what was happening anywhere.

The Council had accomplished what no amount of force had ever achieved, and the people of the world clamored for the shackles that would make slaves of them forever.

With the world's governments scrambling to regain the control that was steadily and rapidly slipping away from them, the Council initiated the final phase.

The Consiglieri had concluded that in order to prevent the devastating levels of corruption from ever rising again, death on a large scale was inevitable. Without an overtly violent direct action phase, suffering could be kept at an absolute minimum, and the plan for that was the most humane ever devised.

Among the most valuable tools in the Tether's arsenal was the discovery of the bioelectric frequencies specific to living things. Every organism had them, and each was unique.

When a counter frequency of sufficient power was focused on a targeted species, it halted all electrical activity. It was, in effect, a biological electromagnetic pulse that turned off life forms instead of machines. It was no surprise to any of Tether's scientists that the frequency that facilitated synapses in human beings differed from all others. It seemed oddly fitting that it should be stronger than that of any other species, making it among the first to be identified and isolated.

The technology, aptly named Switch, was the first weapon implemented. The frequency pulses were fired from space, switching off all human life in the target areas while leaving everything else alive. It focused on population centers of greatest saturation, where most environmental damage originated.

The method proved even more efficient than predicted, with a survival rate of less than three one-hundredths of a percent at ground zero of each primary target area. The only people to survive were those who happened to be outside the targeted area or somehow shielded within it, protected in deep, underground vaults or the few survival bunkers that were sufficiently insulated. There were less than ten witnesses to Switch as it occurred. All described the victims falling simultaneously, like millions of marionettes having their strings cut. The process was assumed to have been painless, but there was no way to verify.

It was important to note that even the best-laid plans often go awry, and the Transition was no exception. The Council suffered two significant setbacks that very nearly caused the Transition to fail. Both originate with the Kadverians. None afield today bore the surname, Jæger or otherwise.

A brother and two sisters of that clan had held highly influential seats in the Council. Unfortunately, all had profound differences of opinion about how certain aspects of the Transition should be carried out.

As one might imagine, plotting the world's end would be a delicate subject in any scenario, deserving of serious and thorough consideration. Accordingly, there had been multiple discussions on what would constitute a sustainable human population and how that population would be monitored and regulated after the fact. The Kadverians viewed these matters harshly, never seeing eye to eye with their fellow Consiglieri. They felt that there should be an element of punishment in the execution of the Transition – if only to serve as an example for all generations of people to come. The discourse was always civil, and it was concluded that the Transition would proceed as planned. The Council assumed, wrongly, that all those opposed had agreed to disagree.

Instead, the Kadverians took it upon themselves to decide not only how many people were to survive... but also how the additional populations must be dispatched. The greater good was all that mattered, and the cost of folly must be branded into the genetic memory of all those who would survive. History does not fault the other Consiglieri for trusting in those closest to them. However, their lack of attention will always be considered a cautionary tale and object lesson in diligence.

While Arlon respected the Kadverian commitment, especially in a time in history when it was so uncommon, such a profound betrayal can never go unpunished. The Kadverian line had, therefore, been summarily rendered extinct. The severity of the retribution visited upon the family was not solely due to the acts themselves but more how they'd gone about them.

The Kadverian Event coincided simultaneously with the Switch. Ledo Kadverian and his twin sister Helena, foremost of the geneticists at Tether, had chosen biowarfare - perhaps the most heinous method in the long, sad history of genocide - as the means of both castigating those who had harmed the Earth and preventing further consideration of ever doing so again.

The weapon came in the form of an altered enzyme that had been extracted from, of all things, the corpse of a captured vampire. The delivery mechanisms had been previously staged, and when the Transition began the substance was introduced into the water supplies of all secondary metropolitan areas in the world that were not targeted by the Switch.

Any given human body contains multiple strains of bacteria, each with its own dedicated purpose. Gut bacteria, essential for digestion, have a secondary mission of consuming the host body upon expiration. The Kadverian enzyme, termed Vacteria, hyper-activated this bacteria in every man, woman, and child in the targeted areas. It had been programmed with a new set of orders: Waiting for death to ring the dinner bell was no longer necessary.

Countless millions of people were eaten alive with the speed and efficiency of an industrial acid. Bodies were rendered skeletal before putrefaction could even set in, and in some cases reduced to dust. The survival rate of the Kadverian Event victims was less than a tenth of a percent overall. It was as effective as the Switch but not nearly as quick - and not at all painless.

The Council realized quickly enough what had happened, and it was obvious where the blame must lie. An accounting was due, and though none had ever disagreed on that point, the genetic deletion of the Kadverian family might never have happened had it not been for the global retaliation that occurred in the wake of the atrocity.

Never in the history of man had any person or group been so enthusiastically pursued. But for the competency and foresight of the Council, not a single member would have survived. Most Scions believed it unlikely that anyone would be left on the planet now in any case, given humanity's pre-Transition trajectory, but that was academic. There certainly must have been suspicions, but the Council had taken extreme care to be nonexistent in the vast digital landscape. They were chameleons, having long since established ironclad control of all levels of the internet, down to the primordial, sub-Marianas bogs where only a few of the most technologically savvy were capable of treading... or dared.

Predictably, the survivors in America responded to the atrocities with particular enthusiasm. Lacking a physical enemy upon whom they might focus their justifiable rage, they did the next best thing. They vented their aggression upon those who'd long established themselves as eminently responsible for most, if not all, of the world's wrongs. The Consiglieri's plans came to poetic fruition as the Church and State found themselves the targets of the black hatred of a large, well-armed, and highly motivated populace.

To say that the planet's survivors were furious at the harm inflicted upon them was an understatement. There is no word in any language that could have done it justice. It was hard to say who was more tenacious, the corrupt or those who inevitably rose to destroy them. Americans, in general, were notoriously spirited folk. They were regarded as utterly, lethally unpredictable by every foreign military to ever face them. If there could have been a worse group of people to find oneself on the wrong side of, Arlon couldn't imagine.

The nation had grown up hard and fast, surviving all manner of external conflicts. They'd faced their share of internal upheaval as well, including one civil and two revolutionary wars during which corrupt governments were ousted.

Their very inception had been brought about by groups of starving men, losing fingers and toes to frostbite, yet still willing to cross frozen rivers in the dead of night to kill an enemy. Some of those battles had raged across the very ground upon which Arlon, Gaither, and their brother and sister Scions now walked. He had all of the documentaries, of course, but there was nothing quite like walking in the literal footsteps of history. For a moment he was tempted to pause and remove his boots to do just that. It made him smile.

More than any other group, Americans would have required vigorous oversight to maintain the new order. Fortunately, many of the original Council were American, born and bred, making them well-suited to the task. Ultimately, it made the Council's decision to headquarters here even better.

As to the mayhem that arose following the opening blows of the Transition, the American governmental response aligned with the Council's forecasted reaction so closely that it could have been scripted. Instead of calling all patriots to come together and repel this new and unprecedented threat, they chose to cover their own sorry asses. Practically overnight, Congress wrote and unanimously approved a bill nullifying their Constitution and declaring martial law. Predictable as sunrise and fools to the last, the American government had burned the last and only bridge that might have saved them.

The last signature was penned on that bill on a Wednesday afternoon. By the early hours of Thursday morning, the third and Last American Revolutionary War was well underway. The attacks were spearheaded by local law enforcement, militias, and what remained of the military. Nearly three-quarters of the U.S. government did not survive to see the sunrise the following Friday morning. The neuroholographies of the collapse and the trials were terrific; even the public executions had been recorded for posterity.

Expectedly, the shrewdest politicians and clergy fled like rats from a burning ship, never to be seen or heard from again. The majority had no contingency plans, however. Amusingly enough, many of these would turn to Tether for aid, advice, and even sanctuary. All were ignored.

Regardless of how the traitorous thieves responded, the predominant sentiment had been indignation. Politicians could not conceive that the peasantry would dare raise arms against their elected leaders. A few even managed to maintain their outrage up to the very moment they were hung or shot, which tickled Arlon to no end. A congressman from California had been the first of these, smirking his way to the gallows, chuckling even as a Staff Sergeant from the National Guard put the hood over his head - like it was some elaborate practical joke they would all soon be laughing about. He soon discovered that immortality was not among the things money could buy.

Like the citizenry at large, those who remained in any government had no clue who their antagonists might be, and therefore found themselves unable to establish contact, covertly or otherwise. Instead, leaders of some of the world's largest and most powerful countries began issuing statements over public social media - like standard television commercials - proclaiming how invaluable they would be as assets. They pledged oaths of loyalty and the full might of their militaries. Notably, and true to form, there was never any mention of sparing their own people.

The Council allowed seven days for the magnitude of the Switch and Kadverian Event to achieve the maximum effect on the worldwide psyche before issuing their one and only communication, the Ultimatum. It was translated into every significant language and broadcast worldwide.

We, the Consiglieri of Tether - formerly the executive leadership of Tether Corporation - congratulate you, the Survivors of the Transition. We commend your resilience and welcome you to the New World.

This body hereby assumes stewardship of this planet in perpetuity, and shall henceforth be regarded as the sole arbiter of acceptable behavior.

The requirements for peaceful coexistence are straightforward.

Remnants of all national governments shall disband immediately and never seek to re-form.

Likewise, military elements of any size or structure are no longer necessary. They shall disarm themselves of all weaponry crew-served and larger and stand down. Those who have served in any military capacity will not be held accountable for the actions of their host governments. Return to your homes and attend to the well-being of those you care for.

The deadline for decentralization and disarmament is forty-eight hours.

From this day forward, all people shall take utmost care to do no further harm to this planet Earth. Specifically, there shall be no production or discharge of toxic materials and/or waste by any entity, nor any other harmful actions that jeopardize the health of the planet and the organisms that dwell upon it. The only exception shall be hunting for consumption, as it has always been necessary for the human species.

These mandates are non-negotiable, and all resistance to these or any that follow will be met with immediate and severe consequences.

The Consiglieri regret the intensity of action required to effect change - the obstacles were formidable - but it is done and cannot be changed. Comply, and you shall all be left to your own ends.

We encourage all to do their best to seek meaning in their existence and live in peace with one another.

There was never a doubt that the entire human race would fight, of course, and fight they did. It is remembered as the Great Unification. For the first time ever, in all of recorded history, differences great and small were cast aside. The remnants of all the world governments pooled their considerable resources.

Three colossal armies began to amass in "secret" locations, ready to smite their common enemy - whose own forces had yet to physically appear. The Consiglieri remained unresponsive to attempts at reestablishing contact, and successfully evaded all efforts to locate them. But for the unprecedented mass extermination for which they'd claimed responsibility, it was as if they didn't exist.

The world could only hold its breath and wait as the clock ticked. Some people hoped or prayed for an outcome that might restore them to the reality they'd so recently known. Most took the advice suggested by the Ultimatum and did their best to distance themselves from the remaining population centers, especially those places that even hinted at a military presence.

Meanwhile, despite an auspicious start, the Coalition Command had quickly reverted to form. With the hourglass slowly running out, Commanders bickered over authority, troop dispositions, and even whether or not this "Council" actually existed - right up to the last grain of sand.

As promised, there was no final warning. At forty-eight hours and seven seconds after the Council's only broadcast, the first and only full-scale military attack commenced. Although the Consiglieri had never planned a physical assault, they were well-prepared to do so. Not since the Younger-Dryas event had the planet experienced such an enormous release of energy. The event was recorded and stored in multiple digital formats. Arlon owned the entire compendium.

Notably, most of the Council's weapons technology was not of human origin but rather the product of reverse-engineered alien technologies. Allegedly, these had been gifted long ago to Earth's amusing little hairless primates out of curiosity... just to see what We would make of them.

Finally deciphered and perfected by Tether, the greatest of these systems were placed into orbit where they'd remained for generations, disguised as harmless communications satellites and hidden amongst the tremendous, growing ring of space junk. Some of these "Big Irons" remained above to this day, left in place to deal with things like rogue planet-killer meteors or unwanted visitors that might eventually decide to revisit. Arlon glanced up at the darkening sky, wondering which twinkles were stars and which were celestial watchdogs. And which was more deadly.

The strikes were simultaneous. All three of the Coalition Armies were obliterated almost instantly. A few hundred thousand soldiers, ships, aircraft, and all weaponry and ammunition reduced to loose atoms in the space of time it takes for a dying man to release a final, rattling breath. The "undetectable" places where they'd staged were now expanses of blackened glass.

Why is this happening? Earth's remaining leaders had demanded of nobody in general. *How could you do this to your own kind?* They were excellent questions, Arlon thought... rhetorical, but excellent. For the answers had always been there, seemingly apparent to any intelligent person who might have cared enough to think it through. The average ten-year-old child in today's world could have explained it to them. The answer was that, in short, there had been no choice.

The months that followed the attacks were a time of experimentation. Even with the annihilation of the militaries, the Consiglieri discovered, to its dismay, that the global population was still unacceptably high. Most disappointingly, they remained prone to extreme violence, much as the recently deleted Kadverians had predicted. Culling was the obvious solution, but how could it be done so that the strongest continued to survive?

Here, the Consiglieri were unknowingly aided once more by the Kadverians. One of the tasks of Tether's geneticists had been to devise a way to "sniff out" those whose DNA would prove valuable in the new world, and find a way they had. They called them Golems - living biological sponges that formed according to their environment, programmed to hunt down all human candidates of sufficient intelligence to be spared.

The project had unfortunately been fraught with problems, an unacceptably sour note in the symphony of transformation, yet the Kadverians regarded it as a diamond in the rough. Rather than destroy their work, they'd left it in place as a contingency plan, a legacy hail Mary should their efforts to augment the Transition fail and prove disastrous. These monsters - for that is what they were - were held in check by means of a dead-man-switch activation system, requiring at least one member of the Kadverian family to postpone the release daily. When the last was executed, the gates opened.

Though the project did serve to locate a fair number of assets, the monsters wrought havoc upon what was left of society, and it took nearly half a century for the Jægers to hunt them to extinction. Allegedly, all but one species were successfully eliminated. Dragons. They were said to remain, existing in the deepest wilds and jungles and preying on anything careless enough to blunder into their territory. Though Arlon was skeptical, it seemed almost impossible to verify. From what he knew of them, encountering one of those creatures was likely to be the final event in a person's life, no matter how skilled or well-armed they might be. As miscalculations went, the results of that experiment could have been worse. Since the end result was achieved, the consensus was that hunting mutations for half a century was a small price to pay for eliminating ancient man as the apex species.

Homo sapiens had since been taxonomically reclassified as Homo inferior, and deservedly so. As an organism, they'd proven only marginally less destructive than viruses and, with few exceptions, had been slowly and most assuredly rendering the world uninhabitable since the Industrial Revolution. Prior to, people had held a more commonsensical approach to living together in numbers. Any person who shits in the village's fresh water supply could not and had ultimately *never been* allowed to maintain control of wells, rocks, or even pointy sticks – much less anything of importance. Those individuals invariably suffered banishment or other fitting form of punishment.

Inexplicably, unacceptable behaviors like these were somehow allowed to become normalized. Once that cycle began, the deterioration of society became only a question of scale and consequences.

It proved impossible to explain any of this to the doomed Homo sapiens. Surely it had been attempted many times, proving that one could never reason with the unreasonable. In large groups, they remained dangerously incompetent and almost always reverted to primitive solutions whenever faced with adversity.

Tribalism was counterproductive to Scion life and the State of the world in general, although shock and awe were still used by Jægers to deal with Inferiori complications. Once a tribe reached a certain number, its people discontinued peaceful assimilation. Violence remained the only dependable catalyst for change within their population, just as fear was the only method of ensuring compliance.

TETHERED

After the Transition, the results of halting the man-made sicknesses plaguing the planet were immediately apparent. With each passing day She'd grown healthier, and was taking ever larger strides toward a return to Her pristine beginnings.

Now and again, there were halfhearted suggestions to extend the Inferiori's freedoms, ostensibly for research purposes. It was posturing and never taken seriously. Arlon was a third-generation member of the Council and, like his peers and predecessors, an avid student of the past. The tribes could never be allowed to grow beyond control. Their ranges must remain restricted, and their numbers carefully maintained.

Even so, Arlon was thankful for their existence. He was among the majority of Scions who subscribed to the notion that the Inferiori should be preserved. They were living reminders of what not to be, but there were also practical evolutionary reasons. Inexplicably, Superiori children were still occasionally born to them, and births in the tribes were carefully monitored, as some Inferiori families were prone to produce highly intelligent offspring. It was hypothesized that these anomalies would eventually breed out naturally, but until that could be verified, the Council would never risk destroying potential assets to the gene pool.

No intelligent being was allowed to raised by Inferiori savages. All such rare, lucky babies birthed into the Tribe were extracted and integrated into a Scion family, where their development could be closely monitored for aberrant behaviors.

Ironically, even though the Inferiori worldwide had a better collective quality of life now than at almost any point in their history, their behaviors did not evolve. Even the smallest groups regularly fought amongst themselves and even murdered one another seemingly without any good reason. It almost seemed they were compelled to do so, as though it were a biological imperative.

The tribes of the Northern Continental Preserve, in particular, still fought with the savage ferocity of the ancient Comanches. Jægers and researchers in equal number traveled here from all over the world for that reason alone. Americans in any age or form, it seemed, simply did not tire of the struggle. Indeed, they seemed to thrive on it. Maybe it was something in the air or the land itself, Arlon mused.

In any case, that tenacity, coupled with the fertility of their females, required commensurate reinforcement, and there was no better means to do so than systematic culling. Arlon would have it no other way.

That Arlon could summarize the world order in the insignificant time it took to cross a small field did not seem remarkable to him. Most of history's grandest tales were the simplest to tell, but any other further consideration of these matters would have to wait. The procession had stopped behind Gaither's Buteo, where a puddle of dark blood had drained through the grating. One of the kills was so fresh that steam yet rose from its shroud into the cool twilight air. It couldn't have been taken longer than three or four hours ago. *What the hell,* Arlon thought with a rueful grimace, *Gait hadn't been kidding, after all.*

Hunting the lands of a conquered people had ever been a privilege of the victorious, and it proved especially gratifying now. It was no easy task to have saved the world and a wondrous responsibility to preserve it. That being said, membership still had its privileges.

Gaither had landed his craft well away from the building to mitigate any potential nosey pre-inspection. He was fond of saying that cheating was wrong, especially in gambling, unless you were one hundred percent sure you could get away with it. Additionally, lovable hypocrite that he was, he'd have certainly set a proximity alarm so that nothing with a bioelectric signature more prominent than a rabbit could get close enough to disturb the kills without activating the Buteo's predator drones.

Arlon eyed the gathering crowd, wondering if anybody had been brave enough to snoop. Most hunters, excepting Gait himself, would never stoop to such a level. In any case, even being his best friend, he would never willingly be the first to approach any of Gaither's vehicles or property alone. The man had a tendency to link all of his alarms to repulsers that would knock a human being flat on their ass.

Gaither was waiting, hand on the cargo gate, puffing small clouds of white breath through that shit-eating grin of his. Plumes of victory dissipating into the cold.

"A'ight-den." Arlon said, in archaic slang. He gestured and crossed his arms. "Lesseeyum."

The gate clanged down with a crash, and one at a time Gaither started throwing back the heavy coverings. The crowd murmured appreciatively, and even Arlon gave a low whistle. *Damn but this guy is good!* He had definitely left it all in the field. Considering the strict regulations that governed culling, it was the most impressive take he'd ever seen.

Three women, seven large men, and four adolescents lay in the bed. All but one were unmarked and looked to be peacefully sleeping. Cull doctrine dictated that kills must be made via Switch-tech weaponry, with several exceptions. Any Jæger attacked first or sufficiently outnumbered could employ any tactics that ensured personal safety. Suffice it to say there were an inordinate number of hunters who "stumbled into ambushes," but Gaither, like most Jægers, had no inner demons that required feeding and, in the main, played by the rules.

There certainly were those who felt no allegiance whatsoever to the hunted, and it often showed in their methodology. These Jægers were exceedingly rare, stone-cold killers who lived alone out on the fringes where the most aggressive Inferiori ranged, and inhumane practices were overlooked.

At the opposite end of that spectrum, Arlon knew Jægers who only hunted Openhand - without weapons of any kind. Laney was plenty good enough to do so, but she loved her guns and blades too much. Openhand was dangerous as hell. The Inferiori might not have the same technology, but there had never been an animal more dangerous to hunt than man.

The procession packed in tightly for a closer look. The trophies were magnificent, healthy specimens, and not one would be considered a waste. Weapons lay beside each of the bodies. Nestled under the arm of one of the women was an aluminum baseball bat, an antique that would likely end up in Gaither's trophy room.

The youngest was a boy of about sixteen, his empty shotgun lying between his legs, breach open. Eyes fixed and open to the sky, he was already stiff with a sparkly coating of frost. That would have been Gaither's first of the day.

Adolescents bearing weapons were fair game, but children below a certain age were never to be purposefully harmed, armed or not. The killing of the very young was barbaric and had always been taboo.

Two of the men were veritable giants, the largest nearly Gaither's size. He'd clearly been taken Openhand; the bone handle of the man's own long knife still protruded from between the ribs under his right arm. *Heart strike. No wonder the puddle was so large.*

Even though he himself would not be partaking in the Rout, Arlon was glad to be a part of it. The Rout was sort of a "world series" of hunts, but Jægers participated in the common culls with fair regularity.

All culls followed uprisings, which in turn were planned and carefully instigated by the Consiglieri. It was a template that worked consistently with little variation. The rage of the Inferiori was kept simmering by the Scionic tendency to live in intimate proximity to them. No proud creature could possibly resist such a deliberate taunt.

While Tribespeople were not terribly intelligent, neither were they necessarily stupid, and Scion anthropologists had devised a brilliant way to capitalize upon that fact. Eventually, even the most feeble-minded clan of Inferiori would eventually come to recognize an unmistakable pattern of never winning or making even the slightest dent in the Superior population.

To mitigate the possibility, the Council periodically staged deaths, preferably a Scion of some import. In most cases, the "dead" Consiglieri family had simply tired of where they lived and volunteered to become sacrifices. The more significant the Scion loss, the greater the victory for the Inferiori cause. Thus far, Arlon's family had been 'killed in action' twice and relocated.

Consequently, Jægers were the only people in history who could not only plan but also *attend* their own funerals. The parties that followed were legendary. Gaither had once given his own eulogy. He arrived late to his own wake, shit-faced drunk, whereupon he commenced to roast himself unmercifully. When he referred to himself as "a hunter nearly as dumb as he was ugly," Arlon had laughed until he cried.

There were legitimate victories, of course, but there had been fewer than ten legitimate KIA in the last seventy years. Most Jægers lost in the field were killed by animal predators like Dire wolves, some species of great American cat, or a rogue bear. The chaotic misfortune of accidents and natural disasters claimed others, and there would always be one or two who perished due to drunken foolhardiness. Even if death were not the temporary setback it now was, the latter would have been considered Darwinian in nature and a contribution to the advancement of the Scion species on the whole.

The Inferiori reacted to their own losses and "victories" in true tribal fashion. The dead were instantly martyred - heroes whose names were added to the great, growing list of those who gave their lives to the struggle. Jægers referred to them as the Martyrs of Irony, and glasses would be raised in their memory for generations to come.

Arlon supposed there would always be an element of one-upmanship to hunting, but for true Jægers, culling was considered an act of mercy. It was necessary, but it didn't have to be cruel. The game were still people, after all... from a certain point of view. It was only right to allow them to fight for their lives if they chose to, and maintain the belief that they might one day overcome their oppression. The odds of a successful revolt were astronomically unlikely, but Scion leadership was nothing if not thorough. Given enough time and opportunity, anything was possible. It was logical to have a contingency plan.

Once again they borrowed from the genius of the Kadverians. High above, well out of sight and mind, were several million drones loaded with enough Vacteria to successfully delete every species of man from the planet forever. They orbited in modified dead-man mode, and at least one member of the Council was required to make contact regularly. Hundreds if not thousands of Scions did so every day, but if ever thirty consecutive days passed with no confirmation, the drones were programmed to descend and blanket the entire planet.

It was ominous information, to be sure, although it didn't worry Arlon in the least. There must be an absolute zero percent chance of ever allowing the world to fall back into the hands of uncaring, incompetent masses. She deserved better.

She'd been saved, and it had taken a group of people, at the time labeled sociopaths, to accomplish it. Elayne would say that the Council, and especially the Jægers among them, were still precisely that, but that it was a necessary quality in anyone who'd ever sought to make change on a global scale. Had the Council not possessed the means and fortitude to act when and how they had, the planet would not have endured, and that's all there was to it. And if the prey ever realized the futility of their struggle? Arlon gave a mental shrug. Even he had to admit that nothing much was likely to come of it.

It was perhaps never fair, but people had been exploited since before the dawn of civilization. They were among the most valuable commodities on Earth, second only to precious metals. The Council was unprecedented in its misuse of humanity in that it had no materialistic motive or narcissistic lust for power. They weren't cruel or evil, nor even wished to cause harm, would that it could have been avoided. They were simply people who'd recognized impending disaster and had possessed the means to prevent it in a logical, scientific way.

A shrill cry sounded above, and Arlon looked up, shielding his eyes against the blue forever until he spotted a pair of hawks circling in search of a meal. He smiled. Most things were as simple as that, coming down to hunter and prey.

He raised an eyebrow at Gaither, and the other gestured permission to address the kills more closely. One was a young brunette just beginning to show with child, still clutching the handle of an axe. He gave a grim chuckle and shook his head at Gaither. "Does that one count as one and a half, Mighty Warrior?" he said with a wink and an extended hand.

"You're damned right it does!" Gaither laughed. "Not that I needed it. I'll have that pass now, if you please." Arlon grinned and grudgingly dug into his pack. He handed it over with grace and dignity, to the immense delight of Gaither's supporters, then turned back to examine the take again.

There might be reasons to end this custom, to be sure, but not near as many as there were to continue. Arlon placed his hand on the woman's chest and bowed his head. *Let them celebrate their losses and victories, and hope in the quiet of their secret places for the day that they might live free once more.*

Perhaps the greatest irony of all time, the Jæger thought, was that they'd *never* been free. And all for the best, really. He prodded a thigh to gauge the muscle tone and nodded approvingly. He sure would miss the hunting.

ABOUT THE AUTHOR

I was born in October of 1969 in Brooklyn Park, Maryland, and was drawing and painting on any available surface as soon as I could reach anything to do it with. By the age of four my artwork was already recognizable, and divided almost equally between monsters and dinosaurs. Those who've known me best would be inclined to say that there has always been something off... at least a little, but none could say that I ever lacked in imagination.

I began writing by accident, and my first real story started off as a hate letter to a car dealership. You could say that it got away from me. I've found the medium of writing to be as rewarding as any visual art I've ever done, which continues to pleasantly surprise me.

My only regret is that I didn't start taking it more seriously a long time ago.

michaelmustachio@protonmail.com

instagram.com/stachelife1112
tiktok.com/@mjmustachio

Made in the USA
Columbia, SC
14 January 2025